More praise for Renata Suerth's
THE WIG: Crazy Summer

"The author manages to truthfully and skillfully get into the head of this precocious girl's consciousness. This book is for every young girl who delights in reading Judy Moody but who is ready for a narrative that tackles some slightly more mature issues."
- Susan Krall, owner of *Off the Beaten Path Bookstore*

"Entertaining and engaging, it's a great read for all ages."
- Cathy Cassani Adams, author *The Self-Aware Parent*

"I love the Grandmother's personality, the tricks Sofia plays on her, and Izzy's honest questions."
- Kate Feutz, middle grade teacher

"THE WIG is a sweet, funny, and endearing story that your elementary aged reader is sure to enjoy."
- Karen Toz, children's author

"I like the theme of the importance of family that runs throughout the book and that Sofie develops a good relationship with her paternal grandmother."
- Anne Grisenthwaite, librarian

For my grandmothers

THE WIG

Crazy Summer

(Book 1)

RENATA SUERTH

All names, places, and events depicted in this book should be considered fictional as they are products of the author's imagination.

No part of this publication may be reproduced, stored in a retrieval system, or transmitted in any form without explicit written permission from the publisher of this work. For information regarding redistribution or to contact the author, write to the publisher at the following address:

website : www.facebook.com/RSuerthAuthor

ISBN/EAN-13 : 978-0-9882685-0-0

First Edition

TABLE OF CONTENTS

1

The News

This is going to be the worst summer of my life! And like with everything, one event leads to another. You just don't expect a bunch of bad ones in a row.

When I heard the news, I headed for the phone and dialed. Depressed, I stared at the huge spider crawling across Mom's French poster of a ballerina. Normally I'd scream. Not this time. I was too shocked by Mom's news. Numb, actually. The phone rang four times before Maggie, my best friend, finally picked it up.

"Hi, Sofie. What's up?" she asked.

Hearing my best friend's voice made me feel even worse. "I have awful news, Maggie." I started sobbing.

"Why are you crying?" Maggie asked.

I took two deep breaths and wiped the tears off my face so I could think better.

"What's wrong? Tell me!" Maggie pleaded.

"You'll never guess. It's the worst news you can imagine," I said.

Silence. Maggie was thinking.

"The worst news you can imagine," I repeated.

"Did somebody die?" she finally asked.

"No." I shook my head, horrified at the thought. Then I added, "It's the second worst thing you can imagine." I was a little annoyed with Maggie's bad guess.

"I don't know what the second worst thing is. What's going on? Tell me!" she pleaded.

"We're moving," I blurted out.

"What?" she asked.

"We're moving in with my grandma...into her house."

"Why?" Maggie asked.

"Well, Mom just told me...she's going back to school...she wants a better job...we need to save money. Can you believe that my parents already sold the house?"

"I didn't know your house was up for sale," Maggie said.

"Yeah, me neither," I replied. I realized that we didn't even have a 'For Sale' sign up or anything.

"They sold the house without telling you? That's horrible!" Maggie gasped.

"You said it. We're moving in two weeks," I added.

"Two weeks?" Maggie repeated.

"Mom wants to go back to school and *I* have to change schools… Fifth grade in a new school! Can you believe it?"

"Change schools? Why? Your grandma lives in Oak Park," Maggie reminded me.

"I know where Grandma Martha lives. We're not moving in with *her*. We're moving in with my dad's mom, Grandma Ursula. Her house is bigger," I told Maggie.

"Where does she live?" Maggie asked.

"In Stevens Point," I answered.

"Where's that?" she asked.

"It's in another state," I said.

"Another state?" she repeated.

"Yes. Wisconsin," I said, sighing.

"Wisconsin?" she repeated.

"It's four hours away," I added.

"Four hours?" *Maggie tends to repeat a lot when she's shocked.* "So you really have to change schools!" she concluded and exhaled really loud.

"That's what I said! Why do you think I'm so upset?" I said, trying hard not to cry again.

The next thirteen days consisted of packing. With every new taped-up box, the house looked emptier and less like our house.

Maggie came over every day to help. Dad didn't want the boxes to be all over the place so he asked us to try to stack them up in each room, in one of the corners. He didn't want things to look any more chaotic than was necessary. So in the living room, Maggie and I made a pyramid out of the boxes. In the dining room, we built a tower. And in the family room, we constructed an igloo. That one was the hardest and the most impressive. (If I knew which box the camera was in I would've taken a picture of the igloo.) Unfortunately, Mom was horrified when she saw her dishes stacked up in our four-box-tower in the dining room. So, she forced us to disassemble all of our monuments.

Since our efforts weren't appreciated, Maggie and I went up to my room to pack.

"You have a lot of stuff," she observed and plopped down on my purple bean bag.

"Yeah, this is endless," I agreed. "I don't know how all this is going to fit in my new room since I have to share it with…"

"You have to share your room with Izzy?" Maggie asked, shocked.

"Oh, I didn't tell you? Yeah, it just gets better every day," I said, sarcastically.

"That's awful. I can't imagine sharing a room with Jack…"

(Jack is Maggie's younger brother.)

"Izzy isn't as annoying as Jack…" I started to say.

"He's not *that* annoying!" Maggie protested.

Maggie looked hurt.

"I mean, all younger siblings are annoying," I explained.

"Yeah," Maggie agreed but still looked hurt.

"I'm sorry. I'm just so mad!"

"It's OK."

"I don't want to move." I said, ready to cry again.

"It's going to be hard at first, I'm sure. But I bet you'll like it there, eventually. Is your grandma...what's her name?" Maggie asked.

"Ursula."

"Is Grandma Ursula nice?" she asked.

"She's OK, I guess," I answered. "She's not as nice as Grandma Martha...I don't know, I only see Grandma Ursula a few times a year."

"I'm sure she'll be great...Is she a good cook, like Grandma Martha?"

"I don't remember," I mumbled.

"I bet she'll do the dance competitions on your X-Box, just like Grandma Martha always did!"

"I don't know." I realized that I did not really know Grandma Ursula at all. I got a little worried.

"I bet she'll make you a great Halloween costume, just like Grandma Martha," Maggie said enthusiastically.

"I have no idea," I said hopelessly. Tears filled my eyes so fast that I couldn't see.

Maggie gave me a huge hug and said, "You'll love Wisconsin. Maybe I can visit you this summer."

"That would be great," I said, trying to swallow the giant lump in my throat.

2

GOOD-BYE OAK PARK

The next morning, Izzy stormed into my room uninvited. "The movers are here!" she announced. I looked out my window and saw a huge truck in front of our house.

"Great," I mumbled. "Why are you so excited about moving to Wisconsin?" I asked. For once, I was actually interested in her answer.

"Because," she replied, unhelpfully.

"Can you be more specific?" I asked, annoyed.

"It'll be fun," she answered.

"Fun? Won't you miss your friends?"

"Yes…but I'll make new ones."

"Did Mom tell you that?" I was suspicious.

"Both Mom *and* Dad said that," she admitted.

"Of course they did. And you think it's that easy?" I asked.

"Why not?"

"Maybe it is…for a five year old. I'm not that optimistic."

"Opti-what?" she asked.

"Nevermind. Can you leave my room and close the door behind you?" I asked.

"Why?" Izzy asked, looking confused.

"Just go. I want to be alone for a minute," I explained. I looked at my lavender room. It never looked so gloomy. It was empty except for my bed. *So this is it.* I shook my head in disbelief. *A two-week notice.* That's all my parents gave me —*just a lousy two-week notice. I feel like I was just fired except I didn't lose a job, I lost my home and my friends – my entire life.*

The four-hour drive seemed like forty hours. Two hundred and forty miles of cornfields, or whatever else grew on this giant boring patch of no-man's-land, was what separated me from my happy life and my iffy future. The drive seemed super long even though I wasn't looking forward to arriving at our destination. Usually, when you're looking forward to something, it takes forever. So, it didn't make sense that this was taking so long. I definitely was not looking forward to temporarily living at Grandma Ursula's. *That's for sure.*

The closer we got to Stevens Point, the worse I felt. The opposite was true for Izzy. The closer we got, the more she wiggled in her booster seat.

"Can you sit still?" I asked.

"No. I'm excited," she answered.

"You will have so much fun," Dad chimed in. "I loved growing up in Wisconsin."

"Think of all the adventures - " Mom started to say.

"I don't want to. I miss my friends." I informed my clueless parents.

"Oh, Sofie, you'll love it. I promise. You just have to be a little open-minded," Mom continued.

Oh is that it? I just have to be a little open-minded? I thought. But out loud I said, "I'll try, but don't get your hopes up... I still don't get why we have to move to another state."

"I already told you," Mom replied.

"Not really. It doesn't make sense. There are lots of colleges near Oak Park. Don't you know that?"

"I know, but this is what we have to do. You'll understand when you're older," Mom said.

I hate when my parents say that. When I'm older, I won't care anymore. And besides, I'm pretty mature for my age. Grandma Martha always says that. I miss her already.

"When are we going to visit Grandma Martha?" I asked.

"We just left…soon…we'll visit her soon. She'll probably want to visit us too," Mom said.

"I doubt it," I mumbled.

"What?" Mom asked.

"Nothing," I answered.

My grandmas aren't exactly the best of friends. They couldn't be more different. Grandma Martha's house always smells like a bakery. Just seeing her house from the street always makes me hungry because I know that inside her kitchen, there's going to be a freshly-baked something waiting for me. Grandma Martha is plump and soft around the waist. When I throw my arms around her, it feels like I'm hugging a goose-down pillow. She smells like freshly-made apple pie. Grandma Martha is always smiling and wears pink lipstick. Grandma Ursula is none *of these things. Like I said, they couldn't be more different. So I didn't envision my poor Grandma Martha driving four long hours just to hang out with Grandma Ursula.*

"There's the exit," Dad announced.

"We're here!" Izzy added and clapped her hands for emphasis.

"Hurray," I added sarcastically. The town looked just like it did the last time we were here. It looked boring.

3

GRANDMA URSULA'S HEADGEAR

When we arrived at the house, Grandma Ursula was standing on her front porch with her arms crossed. Her posture didn't exactly say, "Welcome." Grandma Martha wouldn't be standing on *her* front porch, looking like a sergeant. She'd be running toward us, all excited.

Grandma Ursula was wearing a sleeveless pink housedress with big white buttons going down the whole front of the dress. The dress had two pockets on each side of Grandma Ursula's waist. The pockets wouldn't be noticeable if she hadn't stuffed them with who-knows-what. They were bulging out, giving her figure a weird shape. The fact that she was wearing a housedress and that it was pink made her look *less* like a sergeant, obviously. Whoever heard of a sergeant wearing a pink housedress anyway? Not me. But still, she did manage to look a little scary and weird.

Grandma Ursula was also wearing a wig. *Yes, my grandma wears a wig.* She's been wearing one for a long time. Dad told me that she started wearing it when he was six years old. Obviously, that was way before I was born.

It's a funny story. This is how Dad tells it, "I was racing through the living room when I noticed something furry resting on the couch. I was thrilled because I thought it was a puppy. But when it didn't move, I was devastated because I thought the puppy was dead. And then, for a split second, I was mad at my parents for neglecting to inform me about the newly acquired puppy which, at the moment, appeared to be dead. When I got closer to the couch, I realized that the brown, furry object was not a puppy at all. It was a wig!

He continues, "I became uneasy, wondering if my parents skinned someone to get it. I saw something like that on TV once. Of course I was too young to have watched something like that on TV. Anyway…Horrified, I started to imagine my parents murdering someone with short brown hair and skinning this unsuspecting soul. Or worse, skinning the person alive!" *At this point, Dad pretends to attack me and I scream.*

"Just then," *he continues*, "your grandma stormed into the living room with a giant knife in her hand, announcing that dinner will be ready in two minutes!"

"Well, I almost peed in my pants. Remember, I was only six. I thought I was next," *he tells me laughing*.

"Oh, here's my wig," *Dad says, trying to sound like Grandma*. "God has not been kind to me. So I have to compensate for *His* neglect." *He fluffs up his short hair*.

We both chuckle.

"Is this a wig?" *Dad asks, switching roles. Now he's playing himself at age six.*

This is where I jump in and play the part of Grandma. "Yes," *I answer in a deep voice.*

"W-Where did you get it?" *Dad stammers.*

"In a store. Where do you think?" *I ask in a grandmotherly voice and adjust my imaginary wig.*

"Uhm…a store," *he answers.*

And then we both say, "The End."

And we laugh.

Dad and I performed this skit a million times, seldom in front of an audience, but still. *It's my favorite story from Dad's childhood. As a matter of fact, I love it so much that I decided to make it mine. This new acquisition, a.k.a. Dad's memory, is stored in my brain in the file called,* "Stories To Tell my Children and Other Important People".

Needless to say, I haven't told anyone yet, not even Maggie. But right now, for some reason, I needed to remember the story.

Anyway, Grandma Ursula was still standing on the porch when I finished replaying Dad's childhood horror story. I couldn't help but smile a little. *Maybe I don't know Grandma Ursula that well, but it might be fun to live with her for a little while. She's a little weird but weird could be interesting. It might make the weeks fly by and before I know it I'll be back in Oak Park*, I reassured myself.

"Welcome home," she called from her sturdy, brick porch. Grandma Ursula lived in what's called a Chicago Bungalow. (The Chicago Bungalows are long, brick houses with big basements and an attic. Most of these houses have a big front porch with thick, brick, square columns on both sides of the porch. They look pretty sturdy. They look like they'll be around long after the families who live in them are gone.)

All the houses in our Oak Park neighborhood looked pretty much the same with the only variety being the brick color —some were yellow, some were red, some were brown —and the kinds of flowers the moms planted in the front of each house.

Our house was yellow and Mom planted red roses in the front. My parents finished the basement and expanded the attic so our house was huge. That's the thing about these bungalows, they look modest and small on the outside but are surprisingly big inside.

Most of my friends in Oak Park lived in a Chicago Bungalow and so does Grandma Ursula, except *she* lives in Stevens Point. How this architecture ended up all the way in Stevens Point, Wisconsin, is anyone's guess.

Her house reminded me of Oak Park. *When something reminds you of something else, it brings back memories. I don't know if that's good or bad.*

"Welcome home," Grandma repeated.

Welcome home? This isn't home. I thought of correcting her out loud. Seeing her house didn't make me hungry the way Grandma Martha's house always did and it didn't remind me of a bakery either.

"Hi, Mom," Dad said and they hugged.

"Hi, Grandma!" Izzy jumped out of the car, nearly tripping. Mom and I walked over to Grandma slowly, waiting our turn. We both hugged her at the same time.

"It's good to see you," Grandma said, adjusting her short brown wig.

"You too. Thank you for everything - " Mom started to say.

"Nonsense," Grandma interrupted. "Let's have lunch. Unpacking can wait. I made cabbage soup and potatoes. Who's hungry?"

Silence.

Izzy and I exchanged a look of disgust.

"I am!" Dad spoke out enthusiastically.

The cabbage soup was as good as it sounded. In other words, it was nasty! Izzy and I fished out the potatoes and left the cabbage drowning in the bowl of liquid. As I stared at the limp cabbage floating around, I remembered Grandma Martha's delicious cooking. *Those were the good old days*, I thought. The scent of a bakery was fading.

4

STEVENS POINT

"*R*ise and shine!" an unwelcome voice intruded my quiet room.

"What? But it's summer!" I pointed at the sun shining through the window, as if that was proof of the season. I rubbed my eyes. This was *not* a nightmare and that voice did *not* belong to some drill sergeant. It was Grandma Ursula standing over me, smiling, with her big wig casting a giant ominous shadow on my lavender comforter.

"Well, the day won't wait for you," she warned me while opening the window.

That's OK, I thought. I noticed Izzy's bed was empty. I also noticed the crazy way Dad painted our room. We couldn't agree on the color, of course. Izzy was still stuck in a pink phase and I preferred a more mature color, lavender. So Dad painted the bottom half of our room pink and the top half lavender to make us both happy. We put a giant bookshelf in the room. I arranged my books on the top shelves for practical and aesthetic reasons. So, they're in the lavender territory. But my dresser had to go in the pink zone, for obvious reasons. Oh well. Dad mentioned that we might get bunk beds. That would be perfect but totally unnecessary since *we won't be living here long.*

"Where's Izzy?" I asked.

"Your sister is playing with the kids next door," Grandma answered my question.

"And Mom and Dad?"

"Out on an errand, I suppose."

I looked at Grandma and saw that she was wearing the same housedress she wore yesterday. I noticed that the house didn't smell like cabbage soup anymore but it didn't smell like a bakery either. Actually, it didn't smell like anything. This was weird because everything smelled like something, didn't it?

Grandma Ursula walked downstairs into the kitchen and I followed. The kitchen was nice and bright. It was painted yellow. Every other room in the house, with the exception of the bedroom Izzy and I shared, was painted some shade of grey. *Not too exciting, if you ask me. And not too uplifting either.*

Grandma Ursula's kitchen looked surprisingly modern, for a senior citizen. The chocolate brown kitchen cabinets matched nicely with the white granite countertops. (We didn't even have granite in Oak Park so this was impressive.) The things made out of fabric —

curtains, chair cushions, placemats —were red and white. Overall, it was nicely done.

The rest of the house, well, that's a different story. All around Grandma Ursula's old dark furniture were big stacks of boxes —our belongings. The place looked cluttered. *I don't know why we didn't put some of our stuff in storage.* We didn't have to bring *all* of our things since we weren't staying long. But no one asked me for my opinion, as usual.

Anyway, I plopped down at the round kitchen table and looked around.

"What's for breakfast?" I asked, starving.

"Whatever you prepare, Sofia."

Grandma Martha would make me French toast, I thought.

"The bread is in the pantry and the eggs are in the fridge," she added.

Is she a mind reader? I thought, horrified. I gave her a suspicious look.

"Your sister wanted French toast. I assume you do too," she explained.

What a relief! She's not a mind reader.

"Did Izzy make her own French toast?" I asked, shocked.

"No, your dad made it for her…I only cook once a day…lunch usually. Breakfast and dinner are light. So, you'll have to fend for yourself," she explained.

"That's fine," I said, thinking about yesterday's cabbage soup.

I cracked a couple of eggs. I whisked them and added some milk, a pinch of salt, nutmeg, cinnamon, and paprika (the secret ingredient). I watched Grandma Martha do this a million times. Now I was cooking under the watchful eye of Grandma Ursula, who looked really interested, interested in the finished product, *not* the process.

"You like to cook?" she asked and took a sip of coffee. Her coffee mug said, "I'm not worth a thing before coffee break." It had a picture of Snoopy on it. Snoopy was Charlie Brown's unenthusiastic dog.

"I don't know. This isn't really cooking. I just cracked an egg," I said, like it was no big deal.

"I don't like cooking," she confessed. "Now, your other grandma…she's a great cook."

"Yeah," I agreed sadly, while trying to open the pantry door unsuccessfully.

"The door sticks. You have to pull really hard," she explained. "This is an old house. It's like an old person. You know…half the things don't work."

She chuckled and I smiled.

I submerged a couple of pieces of bread into the egg mixture and threw the slices on the hot pan. A familiar buttery smell filled the kitchen. I closed my eyes and imagined being in Grandma Martha's kitchen instead. I could almost feel her standing next to me. But my sweet daydream was cut short by the abrupt interruption of Grandma Ursula's excited voice, "Yum. That smells good!"

She stood next to me at the stove with Snoopy in her hand and it seemed like they were both watching me. This was a little weird *because how can a comic strip character pictured on a coffee mug watch you?* And another thing that was weird —I think Grandma Ursula was drooling. I've never seen an adult human being drool up close. That wasn't just weird, that was gross!

"Do you want some?" I asked, hoping she'd say no because I was starving.

"Don't mind if I do," she said and took *both* slices. She took a bite and announced, "This is delicious!"

"My first attempt," I confessed, salivating.

"No! Really? Well, you don't take after me in the cooking department. You take after your mom's side," she said, pointing at me with her fork. "Maybe you'll end up on one of these cooking shows when you grow up," she pointed at the small kitchen TV, which I didn't know was on because the volume was low. She got up to turn up the volume. One of her favorite cooking shows was starting. For someone who didn't like to cook, she sure loved to watch other people do it.

I just remembered that yesterday, when she gave us the tour of the house, or rather the rules of the house, she pointed at the kitchen TV and said, "No one is allowed to touch this. It stays on ALL THE

TIME!" The last three words were pronounced a bit louder, for emphasis I suppose.

We all nodded, shrugging. *It's one cooking show after another.*

When the show ended, she pointed at the TV and said, "Sometimes, when the food looks really good, I can almost smell it."

I sat down next to her, intrigued.

"Really? Can you *taste* it too?" I asked, as if the smelling part *was* believable but the tasting, no, that's where I have to draw the line.

"Don't be sassy," she warned, misinterpreting my genuine interest. "You know, it's not that far-fetched. If you can smell something, you can sometimes almost taste it too," she said and pointed at her nose and then her mouth, as if pointing at the body parts explained the phenomenon.

"So you can almost *taste* the food someone's cooking on TV?" I asked, not believing my ears.

"Almost," she replied.

My grandma is nuts, I thought.

Six French toasts later (I couldn't believe Grandma's appetite), Grandma announced, "We need to get some groceries. Can you come with me and help?"

"Sure, I have no plans," I mumbled.

We washed the dishes together because Grandma doesn't have a dishwasher. Then we got into her green Ford Escort and drove off.

"Hey, Grandma, you're not wearing your seatbelt," I said, alarmed.

"It's too constricting," she replied.

"Isn't that against the law in Wisconsin?"

"I don't know," she answered, unfazed.

My grandma is a rebel, I thought, looking at her profile. She could look attractive, even though she's old, if she wasn't wearing her ugly wig. It looks like a brown furry football helmet. Even a semi-blind person could tell that it's fake hair. She might as well wear a clown's wig.

"Why do you wear it?" I asked.

"Wear what?"

"Why do you wear a wig?"

"Oh, I don't know. Some women wear lipstick...others wear a necklace...I wear a wig."

Other grandmas are normal and I'm stuck with a unique dresser, I thought.

"Grandma, do you want everyone to know you're wearing a wig?" I asked.

"What do you mean?"

"Well, nobody's hair is this thick. I mean...look at me! I'm... fifty-five years younger than you and you can see my scalp. Your wig looks a little bit like a football helmet." What I really meant to say was that it looked just like a football helmet but I didn't want to be rude.

"Football? Listen. Stop criticizing! I've been cursed. My sister was the pretty one. She had all the hair too! I've had this baby-thin fuzz on my head my entire life. Sixty-five years! It hasn't been easy."

"Your real hair isn't so bad...Really, why do you wear it?" I pressed on.

Grandma thought for a moment and then said, "Habit...I can't stop now. I'm too old to change...I put my shoes on before I go out...I wear a wig before I go out...I ...Oh, here we are. Help me look for parking. I can't see that well. I forgot my glasses."

"You what? We drove all the way here and you can't see?" I asked, horrified.

"Oh, relax. You sound just like your father. We made it here alive, didn't we?"

That's my grandma - a wig is a must but glasses are optional, especially when you're out driving. I shook my head in disbelief.

When we walked into the grocery store, Grandma headed straight for the deli. She greeted a few of the people in line but didn't take a number, which I thought was odd. *Everyone knows you have to take a number.* When the salesgirl shouted, "fifty-six", the woman holding that number looked at Grandma and said, "You go ahead, ma'am."

"Thank you," Grandma said, squeezing her way through the crowd.

"Wow, that was really nice of that lady to let you cut in front of her!" I said, when we left the deli.

"Yes, wasn't it?" she said, as though this was a common occurance.

We approached another line at the bakery. Same thing happened. Grandma did not take a number. Instead, she greeted a bunch of people again. When the next number was called, everyone offered to let her cut in line.

And guess what happened at the butcher's? Yep, the exact same thing!

Well, I couldn't resist asking, "Grandma, why does everyone let you cut in line?"

"People in Wisconsin are very nice," she answered.

"No, that's not it," I disagreed.

"Of course it is," she said, annoyed. "This is not some suburb of Chicago!"

"Why is everyone so nice to YOU?" I asked, intrigued.

"Why not?" she asked, giving me the evil eye.

Back in the car, mulling over Grandma's choice of headgear, I asked, "So if you wear it now out of habit, why did you start wearing it in the first place?"

"Wear what?" she asked.

"Your wig," I reminded her.

"Boy, you're persistent…Well, I guess I didn't want my balding husband to have more hair than me…I suppose I was a bit annoyed with God for being stingy when he created my hair follicles," she explained.

"So you were just vain?" I asked.

"Watch it!" She gave me a stern look and continued, "No, it wasn't vanity…Besides, what's IN your head is more important than what's ON your head."

"Really? So, why are you wearing the wig, Grandma?" I persisted.

"You're exhausting, Sofia!" she said, throwing her hands up in the air.

She didn't answer my question.

"Let's get these groceries in the house," she continued. "I'll tell you where everything goes."

Grandma stood in the middle of the kitchen like a traffic cop in the middle of the intersection and threw her arms left and right, hollering orders. "No! The cabbage goes in the fridge!"

As I half-listened to her orders, I thought about that wig. My grandma didn't start wearing a wig because she battled cancer and lost her hair through chemotherapy. No, that would be noble and tragic.

Was my grandma just vain? What made this worse was that strangers assumed she had cancer (because no normal person would choose to wear a wig). *I think that's what happened at the grocery store today.* The customers saw the wig and thought *cancer* and responded with pity and kindness. They let her cut in line and Grandma accepted their kind gesture without hesitation, every time.

This kind of stuff would happen on all of our future excursions. Every couple of weeks, Grandma would recruit me to go grocery shopping. We didn't always go to the same store. But wherever we went, the customers would be really helpful and nice to Grandma. For some reason —maybe the size of the city —we hardly ran into anyone she knew (except for the salespeople).

The strangers' kindness would make my curiosity grow and I would bombard Grandma with questions, of course. I would ask, "Why is everyone so nice to *you*?... Why do *we* have to go to different grocery stores every time we go shopping?...Why don't you want to shop in *your* neighborhood and run into *your* neighbors?...Why is everyone letting *you* cut in line?"

Grandma's answers didn't satisfy me. "Why not?...I like variety... I see my neighbors in the neighborhood...People in Wisconsin are nice."

To get me off her back, Grandma would develop little pains here and there. I think she did that to justify the special treatment she got from her fellow shoppers. I should add, that it didn't take long for Grandma to start comparing the kind strangers with the "neglectful invaders" of her home - *us*.

A few weeks after we moved in with Grandma, she announced, completely out of the blue, "You people have no respect for the elderly and ill!"

"Are you sick, Grandma?" I asked, worried.

"It's possible. God only knows." She adjusted her wig. "But that's not the point. I am a senior citizen and nobody here seems to notice that," she stated, putting down her Snoopy coffee mug rather loudly to emphasize her point.

My parents looked at each other, confused. And then, my dad exclaimed, "You know, it's the wig!"

"What?" Grandma asked and adjusted her wig again.

"The wig makes you look a lot younger," he would explain, while pouring coffee into Grandma's mug. This comment would surprise her. I could tell. She would glance at herself in the microwave door and then turn her head left and right, smiling a bit. Then she would go to her room for a minute and return to the kitchen *sans* wig. *Sans* means without, I learned that in French class.

Like I was saying, from that day on —a few weeks into our stay — Grandma would roam around the house without her wig. She would only wear it in public. So Izzy and I would have to get used to having two Grandma Ursulas, *as if one wasn't enough*. The older wig-less version lived with us and the younger, wig-wearing but ill-looking impostor would parade in the streets of Stevens Point, taking advantage of every naïve, well-intentioned stranger.

But, like I said, all of this would happen over the next few weeks. I didn't understand the power of the wig on that first day at Grandma Ursula's. I didn't know that people really thought she was ill and were nice to her for that reason. I also didn't realize that Grandma Ursula knew as much and that's why she shopped all over the place so the kindness wouldn't stop.

As soon as I put all the groceries away, my parents and Izzy appeared in the kitchen. *Good timing!* I thought.

"Well, I have some good news and some bad news," Dad announced. "Which do you want to hear first?"

"The good news!" Izzy hollered.

"No! The bad news," I corrected her.

"Why?" she asked.

"It's better that way," I told her. She looked confused. "It's kind of like eating some gross vegetables first and then your favorite dessert," I explained.

"Oh…the bad news first, Dad," she said, enthusiastically.

Only Izzy can be excited about bad news, I thought.

"I'm going to be gone four long days every week," Dad said, rubbing his temple.

"Why?" I asked.

"Because I got a job…That's the good news!" he announced, smiling.

"Hurray!" Izzy hollered.

"A job?" I asked.

"Already?" Grandma asked.

"Yes! I'm going to teach, full-time. But I'll have to commute to Madison…"

"That's two hours away!" Grandma interrupted.

"I know. That's why I probably won't see you until Friday morning…But we'll have nice long weekends together," he said, enthusiastically.

"Great," I mumbled.

Even Izzy looked a little disappointed, "So I won't see you four days in a row?"

"I'll be home every night but it'll be very late. I'll kiss you good night?" he offered.

"And…Uhm…I signed up for five classes so I can finish my degree," Mom added.

"So you'll be gone too?" I asked, completely shocked. *Our clueless parents are totally abandoning us? I can't believe it! Wasn't it bad enough that they dragged us across the country – to a different state – to live with a grandma we don't know or like much? While my parents are pursuing their dreams, Izzy and I are going to be stuck in this nightmare, all alone in Stevens Point. Well, we'll be with Grandma Ursula but she's part of the nightmare. Who knows what she's really like. I don't know her enough to say. All I know is that she wears a wig and doesn't cook but can eat a ton of food. That's not much to go on, if you ask me, and it's not very reassuring either.*

"You'll be gone too?" I repeated.

"You still have me!" Grandma chimed in, giving me a wink and then she looked at Mom and asked, "Anne, are you still going for that degree in Art History?"

"Yes," Mom answered.

"Is that lucrative?" Grandma asked.

"We hope so," Dad answered for Mom.

"What do you girls want for dinner?" Mom asked, changing the subject.

"We still have some cabbage soup…" Grandma started to say.

I was so horrified at the thought of Grandma's soup that I almost forgot to be sad about my parents' news.

"No!" Izzy screamed. Sometimes it's nice to have a younger sister. I like it when she says what I think. Nobody yells at her for being rude because she's little.

"How about spaghetti with meatballs, garlic bread and brownies for dessert?" Mom asked.

"Yes!" Izzy agreed.

Now, that's a normal meal! I thought. *Mom must feel really guilty about abandoning us.*

After dinner, the phone rang. "It's for you," Grandma announced, handing me the phone.

"Hello. Who is it?" I asked, wondering who knows me in Wisconsin.

"It's me! Maggie!"

"Maggie?" I was thrilled. "What a surprise! What's new?"

"Nothing. I called to see how your first day in Stevens Point was," she answered.

"It's kind of boring so far. When we arrived, Grandma offered us cabbage soup…"

"Gross," Maggie interrupted.

"I know! It was nasty. I almost threw up…How are you?" I asked.

"Fine. I miss you," she said.

"Me too… I miss our house. It didn't smell like cabbage."

Maggie laughed and said, "Listen, my mom said that I can come for a visit in August…before school starts… I could stay a whole week…if it's OK with your parents."

"That's great news! I'm sure it'll be fine. I can't wait 'til August."

5

THE REPLACEMENT

Like I said before, Grandma's been wearing the same wig since my dad was six.

"I get a new one every decade or so," she assured me. But the new one always seemed to be identical to the one she was replacing. *I know because I studied her photo albums.* Like I said before, the wig was a brown furball shaped like a football helmet. *And by brown, I mean poop color. There's just no other way to describe it.*

Grandma's attachment to this wig troubled me because I always thought that variety was important, especially when it pertained to other people. So, after Grandma finished her favorite breakfast — French toast —I asked, "Grandma, why don't you change it up a bit?"

"I like French toast and you're a good cook," she answered.

"No, not your breakfast…your hair. You know, go blonde or something?" I suggested.

"Blonde? That's ridiculous," she responded.

"Well, the nice thing about wigs is that you can change drastically and instantly…"

"I don't like change, especially drastic and instant."

"You could be a new, exciting person!"

"Exciting? Why? That's ridiculous!"

Grandma was a creature of habit. You could even say that she was stubborn. So I decided to help and recruited Izzy. I emptied my piggy bank. *Grandma can thank me later*, I thought.

Izzy and I walked to town. We couldn't find a wig store so we went to a hat store instead. *Close enough.*

"I'd like to see your wigs, please," I announced, as we entered the store.

"Excuse me?" the salesman looked puzzled.

"You know, fake hair," I clarified. "Don't you sell wigs?"

"No dear. We sell hats," he said, pointing at one.

"Both go on your head…" Izzy interrupted.

Good observation, I thought.

"Well, yes, but they're entirely different products," he informed us. "Why don't you ladies go to the costume shop at the end of the block?" he suggested.

"Yes, let's go there!" Izzy said, bouncing up and down.

I turned to her and said, "You're not getting anything! Remember, we're getting a wig for Grandma. Got it?"

"I know," she assured me, nodding.

"Thanks," I said to the salesman and we left.

Well, the costume shop had wigs alright: rainbow-colored clown wigs, green ones, purple, pink, white, yellow, blue, and even long black ones. There was no brown wig in the entire store. "I don't think Grandma gets her wigs here," I said to Izzy.

"Me neither. Let's try some on," she suggested, jumping up and down.

"You go ahead," I said, annoyed. She disappeared. I knew she wouldn't be much help. *Why did I bring her along?* I wondered.

"Look!" Izzy reappeared, pulling on my T-shirt. She was wearing a black, shoulder-length wig with just a hint of pink highlights.

I wouldn't mind wearing that myself, I thought.

"Not bad. Hold on to it. I think it's the one," I said and emptied out my pockets. I had to make sure we had enough money. The price was pretty steep - $19.99. *But that's OK. Our generosity will be appreciated and that's what counts.*

The pretty saleslady was wearing an attractive long blonde wig herself. She approved our choice, but not so much the recipient.

"The wig's *not* for you? It's for your grandma?" she asked, looking a bit surprised.

"Yes, it's for our grandma," I answered confidently. *What does this woman know anyway?*

Grandma made it clear that she *did not* want to be a blonde. *So, this stylish black wig will be a good compromise. It will be a pleasant surprise*, I predicted.

"WHAT IN GOD'S NAME IS THIS?" Grandma shrieked and pointed at our new black centerpiece on the breakfast table.

"A replacement," I said, proudly.

"A replacement for the beautiful bouquet of flowers that was here yesterday?" she asked, looking horrified.

"No, Grandma, don't be silly. It's a replacement for a wig," Izzy said, smiling.

"And what *wig* is this horror supposed to replace?" she asked, looking around the kitchen as if a bunch of wigs just happened to be dangling from the kitchen cabinets.

The wig on your head? I thought.

"Uhm…yours," Izzy said and pointed at Grandma's head.

"Have you lost your mind?" Grandma asked, looking at me and then at Izzy.

"No," I answered for both of us.

"Well, my dears, why don't you march right back to where you found this…this horse's tail…and beg them for a refund!"

Grandma was fuming.

"But, it's for you," I reminded her carefully.

"And what am I supposed to do with it?" she continued. "Are these pink stripes?" she gasped, her eyes bulging out.

"You're supposed to wear it…They're not stripes. They're highlights, Grandma. It's very fashionable," Izzy answered

I decided to keep quiet.

Maybe this wasn't such a good idea, I thought.

"Good morning ladies!" Dad came in to get some coffee.

"Have you seen what the girls brought home?" Grandma asked, throwing her hands up in the air.

"Not yet, Mom…"

"That!" She pointed at our new furry centerpiece.

"Is it alive?" Dad asked, smiling.

"No," I answered, suppressing a chuckle.

"Don't encourage them," Grandma warned Dad, glaring at him and pointing at us.

"Girls, did I ever tell you about the time when Grandma brought home her first wig? I think I was six…"

"That's it!" Grandma stormed out of the kitchen.

Dad picked up the wig, put it on, and said, "It's a little tight."

"You look good, Dad," I lied and we all burst out laughing. Not only did Dad look hilarious wearing a woman's wig, he looked like Grandma, a younger male version of Grandma. This was both funny and weird.

"OK. Let's be serious," Dad said. He took off the wig to show us he meant business. "Try not to annoy Grandma. Remember, we're living in her house. We need to show our appreciation…"

"That's why we got the wig…," I started to say.

"Well, Grandma is very particular and this wig is not exactly something a sixty-five year old would wear…Why don't you girls keep it for Halloween or something. Doesn't that sound like a good idea?" he asked.

"I get it this year!" Izzy announced quickly.

"Whatever," I said, annoyed that I didn't think of it first. "Then I get to wear it until Halloween!" I yelled and yanked the wig out of her hands. I ran out with Izzy at my heels. I put the wig on as I ran. I looked back to see how close she was getting when I slammed into someone. I fell down, face first.

"Nice wig," I heard an unfamiliar voice. "Who's your friend Izzy?"

"She's not my friend…This is my annoying sister," Izzy informed him.

I got up and looked at the boy talking to Izzy. He looked really cute.

My face felt like a four hundred degree oven.

He had light blue eyes and dark brown hair, a combination you don't see that often. He was a couple inches taller than me and had nice muscles. He was wearing faded jeans but wasn't wearing a T-shirt. That's how I knew about the nice muscles. His chest looked like a sculpture I saw in one of Mom's art books. No, wait, he looked like a movie star. *Imagine, a movie star living in Stevens Point, Wisconsin*. Who would've thought.

I couldn't speak. On top of that, my arms wouldn't move, so I couldn't get the stupid wig off my head. But that didn't matter because my sister came to my rescue, even though that was not her goal —to rescue me. She yanked the wig off my head and ran.

The boy just stood there looking at me. The tiniest smile was forming on his lips. He bit them and it was gone. I tried not to think about what I looked like.

"My name is Andrew."

"I…I'm Sofia," I stammered.

"I live next door. Izzy's been playing with my sister this whole week. You must've just moved here?" he asked.

"Yeah…but it's temporary," I said, trying to sound as nonchalant as possible.

"You have a leaf stuck to your forehead," he said, pointing at his forehead.

"Oh, thanks," I chuckled, completely horrified.

"See ya," he said and walked away confidently. *He even walks like a movie star*, I thought.

I just stood there, stuck. It was as though I sprouted roots.

Izzy came running back, disappointed that I wasn't chasing her. She opened her mouth to say something but I spoke first, "The wig's yours."

6

THE LESSON

I'm in love.

I spent most of the last three days in Grandma's bleak bedroom, looking at Andrew's house. I haven't seen him since the wig encounter. Being new in town, I had to be careful about the impressions I made, especially when a cute boy was involved. *Next time I see Andrew, I want it to be memorable, but in a good way.*

Grandma's bedroom was the best place to spy, I mean watch, because her large windows faced his house. Plus her long, dark curtains were perfect for my little surveillance. I could hide behind them easily. Her entire room was so dark —dark gray to be exact — that if I wasn't conducting my important investigation, I wouldn't be in it. The only bright thing in Grandma's room was her Styrofoam head. (I had to capitalize Styrofoam because it's a brand name like

Band-Aid or Kleenex.) Grandma always put her wig on the Styrofoam head when she wasn't wearing it. The thing looked eerie both with and without the wig. It was so white that it almost glowed in the dark. If I didn't know any better, I'd think it was staring at me.

"Are you in my room again?" Grandma called from the foyer.

"Uhm…I'm cleaning your room…I'm dusting," I lied.

"Nevermind that. I don't want you to break something. Out! Out! My room's off limits. Why don't you go outside and play with your sister. She's bored."

If I'm gonna go outside, I have to change, I thought. *What if I run into Andrew? I must look perfect.*

It took a few minutes to pick out the perfect outfit. I polished it off with mom's lipstick. Finally, I was presentable. I went outside to find Izzy.

"What's that on your lips?" Izzy asked, making a gross face. "Are you wearing mom's lipstick?"

"No," I lied.

"Why are you so dressed up?"

"I'm not," I said, and looked at my elegant, somewhat tight, knee-length, denim skirt; my elbow-length white blouse; and my very fashionable black, diamond-studded flip-flops.

"Yes you are," Izzy disagreed.

"Let's go outside," I suggested, ignoring her observation.

"Why?"

"Do you want to learn how to ride a bike?"

"Yes!" she squealed.

"Let's go," I said.

"Don't you want to change?" she asked and pointed at my outfit.

"I just did...I mean... No. Listen. I'm not gonna ask you again. Do you or do you not want to learn how to ride a bike? You're too old for training wheels." I pointed at her small pink bike with training wheels. "You can borrow my bike. It's too small for me anyway."

That was a tiny lie. My bike wasn't too small for me. It was the perfect size for a ten year old which probably made it too big for a five year old. That little fact didn't concern me at the moment because I just couldn't think of anything else we could do in front of Andrew's house.

"Fine, I'll get my helmet," she said and disappeared into the garage.

I got my sunglasses so I could observe Andrew without him knowing that I was watching. I didn't want him to think that I was a stalker because, obviously, I wasn't.

"Alright, ready?" I asked, facing Izzy but secretly looking at Andrew's house.

"What's with the sunglasses?" my meddling sister asked.

"It's sunny."

"No it's not."

"Listen. I'm doing you a big favor here. Do you want to stand here and talk or do you want to learn something you should know by now," I said, trying to shame my sister into obeying me.

"OK. Let's go. But you look like a freak!"

Normally, such talk would get my sister in trouble. Since Andrew could be watching, I couldn't push her off my bike or hit her, even though that's exactly what she deserved. Instead, I took a deep breath and straightened out my clean, white blouse. *Punishment can wait*, I thought.

"OK. I'm going to walk with you and hold your seat. So, don't worry. You just pedal and steer," I told her.

"You won't let go?" she asked, nervously.

I noticed that her legs barely reached the pedals. "No," I assured her and I really meant it. I just didn't expect the minor distraction (or the horrifying consequence) which was about to occur.

A yellow convertible drove up the street and the kids inside were hollering. Andrew was one of them. He stood up in the backseat, shouting and waving at us. I couldn't hear what he was hollering about but I was glad I looked great.

I waved back, letting go of the bicycle for a second. Izzy was on her own. Did I forget to mention that grandma's house was on a slight hill? It's nothing you'd notice until it was too late, like now.

I watched my helpless little sister barreling down the hill, away from me. I was paralyzed with fear. I couldn't yell or move. She was screaming her head off.

"Use the breaks!" someone yelled from the convertible.

I don't think she heard because she wasn't slowing down.

I snapped out of my temporary paralysis and started running after her. *My poor little sister is going to die! She's going to die and it's all my fault. She's going to die and then my parents will kill me!*

I noticed that I wasn't running very fast. I realized what the problem was - my stupid, fitted skirt. I did the unthinkable. I pulled the entire skirt up to my waist, completely exposing my purple underwear. *So much for dressing up,* I thought. And I ran. I've never run so fast in my entire life.

I looked to see what awaited us at the bottom of the hill. It was some kind of a forest preserve. *And you know what that means! Trees. Lots of trees.* Knowing Izzy, she'd slam into the biggest tree in the entire forest. Not on purpose, of course. But that's just how she is.

The people in the car drove to the bottom of the hill, way ahead of Izzy. They stopped the car and got out. They lined up next to each other and made, for lack of a better word, a human fence. They looked like they were ready to catch her. *That was pretty courageous,* I thought later that night when I was replaying this nightmare in my head. I was only a few feet behind Izzy and we were approaching the human fence fast. So I was really thankful that Andrew's friends were so brave and decided to buffer Izzy's impact.

Someone yelled again, "Use the breaks!"

She did.

I didn't expect her to slow down so suddenly. So, I ran into her and we hurled into the human fence. At least we weren't going 50 miles per hour anymore because Izzy finally used the breaks.

It was really quiet for a second.

Then, I heard some moans, some of them were my own.

"Did anyone break anything?" someone asked.

"I lost my flip-flops," I announced, looking at my feet.

"I'm bleeding," Izzy whimpered. Her arms and legs were all scratched up but she was alive.

Thank God! I'm going to be really nice to my sister from now on, I thought. *Or at least for a really long time. Definitely a week.*

When we all got up, we looked to make sure we still had all of our body parts. Luckily, no one lost a limb.

"Sofia, you run pretty fast…when you're not wearing a skirt," Andrew said, dusting off his t-shirt.

I realized that my entire skirt was still all the way up at my waist. I was standing in the middle of the street in my underwear. My face got really hot. I've never been so embarrassed in my entire life. *If only I could turn into an insect and fly away,* I thought.

"You should try out for track," he continued. "Seriously, you're fast."

"I was running downhill," I replied, pulling my skirt to where it should be.

Andrew looked at Izzy and said, "You know, that bike is too big for you. You shouldn't be riding it, especially downhill."

"I know," Izzy replied and glared at me.

"WHAT IN GOD'S NAME HAPPENED TO YOU?" Grandma shrieked when we collapsed on the front porch. She was snoozing in her rocking chair.

"You told me to just pedal and steer," Izzy wailed, looking at me. "You said you weren't letting go!"

"I'm so sorry…," I started to say.

"You fell off a bike?" Grandma asked, looking confused.

"Sofia let go of me and I almost died!" Izzy cried.

"You need to get cleaned up. Follow me…both of you," Grandma said, glaring at me.

That night I had two nightmares. In one, Izzy was the main character. She was sitting on a runaway skateboard and I couldn't save her. *The weird thing is that we don't even have a skateboard.* I woke up completely out of breath.

My other nightmare involved the citizens of Stevens Point. They were walking around town in their underwear.

I don't know which nightmare was worse.

The next day Izzy didn't talk to me, at least not directly. She talked to me *through* Grandma. That became annoying real fast.

At breakfast, Izzy announced, "Grandma, can you tell my sister that I don't want French toast today? I have a taste for pancakes." She may have been addressing Grandma, but she was looking straight at *me* the whole time.

Grandma, not thrilled with her new role as messenger, looked at me and said, "Did you hear that, Sofia? Your injured sister wants pancakes...But not me, I still want my French toast."

I was still so shook up from yesterday that I just nodded and got to work.

"Grandma, can you tell my sister that I'd like a strawberry shake with my pancakes?" Izzy announced.

"And one strawberry shake," Grandma added, rolling her eyes.

"Coming up," I mumbled.

"I would also like a fruit salad, Grandma," Izzy added to her breakfast order.

"She wants a salad too," Grandma added, frowning.

"Not a salad! A fruit salad," Izzy corrected her.

"A fruit salad...Where are you going to put all this food?" Grandma asked, looking at Izzy.

"In my stomach," she answered.

"Don't get smart with me, Missy! Just because you had a little accident doesn't mean you can terrorize your entire family with your demands..."

"It was a big accident! I could've died!" Izzy whined. She looked like she was about to cry.

"But you didn't. You're still here and you're bossing everyone around. Next time you'll be more careful," Grandma said.

"But I was…Sofia got distracted by Andrew and she let go of me," Izzy said, frowning.

"Your pancakes are ready," I announced, changing the subject.

"Yum!" Izzy said, looking happy again.

It doesn't take much to make a kid happy, I thought.

A couple of minutes later, I gave Grandma her French toast. She took a bite and said, "Yum!"

I guess it doesn't take much to make an adult happy either.

7

THE TORCH

We moved to Stevens Point a month ago and I haven't met anyone my age except Andrew. And our encounters weren't exactly positive. Before the underwear incident, I was dying to "run" into him and that made me pretty busy. Choosing outfits and looking fabulous is time consuming. Now, I'm avoiding him like the plague and this requires less effort.

That's why I've been so bored lately. *I miss Maggie.* Being bored without a friend stinks. Boredom, like bad news, is easier if you can share it with someone. When Maggie and I were bored in the summer, we always snapped out of it somehow. One of us would start laughing at something dumb, the other would join in, and soon we were out of control.

So, it was on one of these boring Stevens Point days, when Izzy was off playing with the neighbor, that I got in trouble again.

Grandma was taking a shower and I noticed her wig resting on the couch. I thought about what the firemen said at our last school assembly in May and became intrigued.

Would a wig burn? I wondered.

I went to the kitchen and looked for matches. When the firemen warned, "Don't play with matches," they were obviously just talking to the younger kids, not the fourth-graders. And I wouldn't dare play with matches anyway. I know better. I planned on lighting only one match and conducting a little scientific experiment. *Grandma will never know,* I predicted.

With matches in hand, I hopped back to the couch and lit one match. I made a fist with my other hand and put it in the wig so I could pick it up. I wanted to know how close the match would have to be for one single piece of hair to shrivel up and burn. I never got to find out because I sneezed. *And when you sneeze, you close your eyes. So I don't know what happened. I missed the whole thing.* But somehow I managed to blow out the match with my sneeze and ignite the wig instead. Did I mention that my fist was holding up the wig?

"Ahhhhh! Help!" I screamed. But no one was home except Grandma who, as I said, was in the shower.

With flame in hand, I raced like an Olympic hopeful to the bathroom. But the wind only worsened the situation.

I could hear Grandma ask, "Do I smell burning plastic?"

Her question was answered that very second because I stormed into the bathroom with my torch. The last thing I remember is seeing her naked. Then I passed out.

When I regained consciousness, I was surrounded by: my livid mom, my annoyed grandma, an upset fireman, a scary policeman, a relieved paramedic, my nosey sister, her friend, and Andrew.

Why is Andrew here? I wondered, horrified. *He must think I'm nuts.*

"Boy, you really did it this time," Izzy said, smirking.

"Do you have any idea…," Mom started to shout.

I closed my eyes to blink and decided to keep them closed. It was safer. I could only imagine the questions forming in Mom's head.

One of the strangers came to my rescue and told Mom, "Take it easy. Let her recuperate."

She didn't say another word. Or maybe she did, but I wasn't listening.

8

ANOTHER REPLACEMENT

"Well, someone has to get me a replacement. I can't go out like this," Grandma said, pointing at her head at the breakfast table the next morning.

"Mom, you look fine," Dad said.

"I am *not* stepping out of this house until someone buys me another wig," Grandma said, glaring at me.

"Well, you could try the black wig I - " I offered.

"Absolutely not!" Grandma barked back. "Over my dead body!"

"I'll see if I can get one today after my class," Mom offered.

"That would be nice. I want the exact same one. Wait, let me get a picture."

"That's not necessary. I remember what it looks like - " Mom started to say.

"Nonsense. I'll be right back," Grandma answered and hurried away.

She came back into the kitchen with a very old black & white photo of herself wearing the wig. "Here," she handed the photo to Mom, and said, "I need one just like it."

After breakfast, everyone left. And by that I mean everyone except Grandma and me. I had to stay home and recuperate. Grandma chose to stay home because her wig was now the property of the Stevens Point Fire Department. *I wonder if they'll use it as a prop for their cautionary tales.*

We were both stuck at home. Normally, this would be fine because Grandma was unintentionally pretty entertaining. But not today. Today she was in a foul mood. She was stuck at home because she didn't have her hairdo and it was entirely my fault. She glared at me all day to emphasize this point. When she spoke, she was strangely polite.

"Dear, would you please be so kind and chew with your mouth closed? It's rather unpleasant," she said at lunch.

This didn't sound like Grandma at all. She never said *please,* especially to me. And she never, ever, called me Dear. *I think she was being sarcastic but I didn't dare ask.*

I couldn't wait for Mom to come home with Grandma's replacement. Eight hours can feel like eternity, *especially if you're in jail and the warden is mad at you.*

Just to be safe, I decided to hide out in my room. Whenever I heard Grandma roaming around in the hallway, I pretended to sleep.

With nothing to do but lie in bed, I replayed the burning wig nightmare in my head a few times. I could've lost my hand, burned it to a crisp, with nothing but five little bones sticking out. Luckily, it would've been my left hand, so I could still write and do stuff. But still. That was close.

Then I started to think about Grandma, about the way she looked when I stormed into the bathroom. Her entire body was wrinkled. That was a shock. I don't know why, but I always thought that it was just the exposed body parts on old people that were wrinkled, you know, the face, the neck and the arms. Was I wrong! She looked like a bed sheet that was left in the dryer too long.

Oh, and don't let me get started on her *you-know-whats*. Weren't *they* supposed to be somewhere up around her armpits? Grandma's decided to move, or rather stretch way down, almost all the way to her belly button. At least I assumed she had a belly button. I couldn't see it because of all the extra skin around her waist.

Anyway, that was not at all how I imagined Grandma to look. Not that I ever thought about her in the nude before. *Now I can't stop. I wish I could delete that memory.*

When my parents finally came home in the evening, I ran down to the kitchen.

I heard Grandma ask rather loudly, "They stopped manufacturing it?"

"I'm afraid - " Mom tried to answer.

"No!" Grandma gasped, glaring at me.

It wasn't my fault Grandma seemed to be the only customer.

"Haven't they been making this style for at least forty years?" Dad asked.

"I should have stocked up. What was I thinking? What am I going to do?" she pleaded.

I snuck out of the room to go to the hall closet.

"Well," I heard Dad say, "This looks pretty close, Mom."

"Nonsense! It's too long, too straight, and too dark!" Grandma protested.

I walked in modeling the black wig Izzy and I bought a few weeks ago in the costume shop.

"Oh, no! It looks like that!" she exclaimed, pointing at me.

Mom and Dad looked at me and smiled.

"Yours doesn't have pink highlights, Grandma," I pointed out.

Well, my parents lost it. They burst out laughing. They were laughing so hard they shook.

Grandma took the wig Mom bought and put it on. "See? Ridiculous! Look at us," she said, annoyed.

My parents were still laughing.

Grandma looked at me and said, "Your parents are impossible. How do you put up with them?" She put the wig on and looked in the mirror.

"It looks a lot like your old wig, Grandma," I assured her, stretching the truth a little.

"It's not the same," she replied.

"No, but it's very close. It's only an inch longer and only a shade darker," I said.

At least it looks a little less like a football helmet, I thought. *And the color is a major improvement too.*

"Well, I have no choice. It'll have to do," she said, fluffing the wig up a little.

I think she really liked her new wig. She never admitted that but she also never missed a chance to glance at herself in the mirror, the microwave door, or the occasional store window.

For the first week, I don't think she took it off when she went to bed because it looked really messy in the morning. I felt obligated to state my concern because I didn't want her to ruin her wig. It was, after all, kind of my fault.

"Grandma, do you take your wig off when you go to bed?" I asked cautiously.

"Of course. Why?" She looked at me suspiciously.

"It looked kind of messy the other day, in the morning. I was just wondering," I explained.

"I fell asleep in it once or twice...Don't worry, I'm just trying to get used to it," she replied and fluffed it up a little.

9

THE BOMB

One simple word can have the effect of a bomb going off and destroying its surrounding. I'll get to that word later.

But first, a few days after the torch incident, Mom looked at my hand and said, "Your hand healed pretty well." She cleared her throat and added, "I found a piano teacher for you."

"A what?" I asked. "But I don't want to take lessons anymore," I informed my mom.

"What hobby do you want to pursue? Pyromania?" she asked.

"What's that?" I asked, curious. It sounded more interesting than piano lessons.

"Starting fires," she replied.

Very funny, I thought. "I won't light another match. I promise," I pleaded.

"You need some structure and discipline in your life right now, sweetie."

"No I don't…Besides, why start with a new teacher. What's the point? We're only here temporarily," I reminded my mom.

"I don't know how long we'll live here, Sofie. We may be here for a long time," she said.

"Why? We're going back to Oak Park soon. You said - "

"Listen. We won't be moving back anytime soon…We…we lost the house. We didn't sell it, Sofie," she confessed.

"Huh?" I almost fell off my chair. "What do you mean lost, Mom?"

"It's called a foreclosure," she informed me.

"A foreclosure?" This is when the bomb went off in my head, figuratively speaking, of course.

"A foreclosure?" I repeated. Foreclosures were constantly on the news so I knew exactly what that meant. I just never thought we'd be one of *those* families. *Now we'll never move back to Oak Park.*

"What?" I asked.

"Your dad was laid off last September. He thought he could get another job but he couldn't find one. And the bills just kept coming… It's a miracle that he found a teaching position in Madison," Mom explained.

"Dad was without work the entire school year? Where did he go every day?" I asked, curious.

"He was looking every day. Sometimes he was hired as a substitute teacher. But that was just not enough," she said.

"When were you going to tell me all this?" I asked, hurt.

"We didn't want you to worry," she said, squeezing my hand.

"Does Grandma Ursula know?"

"Yes."

"And Grandma Martha?"

"They both know...Don't tell Izzy anything. She's too little... Don't worry, Sofie. Everything's going to be fine," Mom said, hugging me. "When school starts, you'll meet lots of new friends. You won't be so bored. Soon, you won't miss Oak Park."

I doubt that, I thought. *I will always miss Oak Park.*

She looked a little worried, so I agreed and said, "OK, Mom."

"I love you Sofie."

"I love you too."

10

THE MRS. WHAT?

*T*he next day, after breakfast, Mom said, "Sofie, your new piano teacher's house is only five blocks away."

"My what?" I forgot about our talk last night. Now it was all coming back to me. *Foreclosure. Good-bye Oak Park. Good-bye Maggie. Good-bye Grandma Martha. Hello Stevens Point. Hello Grandma Ursula. And the icing on this lousy cake? A new piano teacher.*

"You can walk to your new piano teacher's house," Mom explained, smiling.

"I have to walk to her house?" I almost choked on my bagel.

"I can't drive you. I'll be in class."

"Can't she come here?"

"She's too old to drive."

"How old is she?"

"I don't know. She's retired."

"I don't want to walk," I complained.

"You can borrow my bike," Izzy offered.

Always eavesdropping, I thought.

"Are you kidding? Your pink bike with training wheels? It's too small. I'll look like a freak," I said to Izzy.

"Who's looking?" the brat snickered. "Andrew is away at camp for two weeks," she informed me.

If Mom wasn't there, I'd hit my sister. But instead, I said, "Stay out of it!"

"Maybe Izzy can walk with you," Mom suggested.

"No thanks," I replied.

"Your loss," Izzy said.

I glared at her.

"Well, think about it Sofie. It might be nice to have a familiar face there on your first day," Mom suggested.

"We'll see," I said.

"And don't be late. It starts today, at 3 P.M." Mom informed me.

"Today?"

"What starts at 3?" Grandma asked, heading for the coffee.

"Sofie's piano lesson. I found a teacher for her," Mom announced proudly.

"That's great! Who?" Grandma asked.

"Mrs. Fingerschnitzel," Mom answered.

"What kind of a name is that?" Izzy asked, but no one paid her any attention.

"Fingerschnitzel? I see," Grandma said, frowning.

"Why are you frowning, Grandma…Is she evil?" I asked, concerned.

"I don't know her enough to say," she replied, pouring cream into her coffee.

I wasn't convinced. *Grandma* always *has an opinion, especially about other people.*

"Maybe she's a witch," Izzy suggested, making a scary face.

"You're not helping," I told her, shaking my head.

"I thought she's deaf," Grandma continued.

"Deaf? She seemed fine on the phone," Mom said, looking a little worried.

"Well, every time I see her at the store and say 'hello', she doesn't respond. I assumed she's deaf. Maybe she's just rude," Grandma concluded, still frowning.

"So, you don't know if she's mean?" I persisted. I was a little worried. Flashbacks of my old piano teacher, a.k.a. the dictator, came back to me. I spent half of each lesson doing scales until my fingers were so numb that I couldn't play my assignment. My teacher was constantly pointing out my mistakes and never, ever, complimented me. Wait, no, I'm wrong. Once, she told my mom, "Sofie has potential." Yep, she gave me one compliment in three years. One good thing about leaving Oak Park — my piano teacher stayed behind.

"Sofie, give this woman a chance," Mom pleaded. "She lives nearby."

"Fine," I said. I crossed my arms and exhaled loudly to show my mom what a huge sacrifice I was making.

"But let me know if you think she's hard-of-hearing, OK?"

"I will," I said, thrilled at the possibility of sabotaging Mom's quest for live music at home (at my expense).

"I will definitely let you know if Mrs. Finger…Finger…What's her name?" I finally asked.

"Mrs. Fingerschnitzel."

"Isn't a schnitzel some kind of food?" I asked.

"Yes, it's breaded chicken." Mom explained.

"So, her name is Fingerbreadedchicken?" I asked.

"Ha, haa! Your piano teacher's name is Fingerbreadedchicken?" Izzy burst out laughing. "So her fingers look like breaded chicken? So she has fat fingers? How could she play the piano?"

For once, Izzy's questions were completely valid but they remained unanswered.

"That's enough," Mom told Izzy and gave her a hug.

Maybe she just has a weird name. It's not her fault. I tried to reassure myself.

11

THE RIGHT HOUSE

I decided to let Izzy come with me, just in case. The woman could be a lunatic. Mom didn't even meet her. In Oak Park, Mom would do a background check on anyone who came into contact with us. In Stevens Point, she was sending us into the unknown...*I think her motherly instincts are slipping.*

"Are you scared?" Izzy asked when we stepped out of the house at 2:45 P.M.

"No. Why?" I asked nervously.

" 'Cause. You look scared."

"If you're going to say stupid things, go back home," I said.

"Fine, I'll be quiet." We walked in silence for four and a half blocks.

"That's the house! Number forty!" she announced, pointing at a pretty blue house with a white picket fence.

"You're right," I said, relieved. *I believe that one's home is a reflection of one's personality. In other words, the occupant of a nice house has got to be nice.*

I knocked on the door and a woman, who did *not* look retired, answered.

"Hello girls, are you selling something?" she asked, smiling.

"No, I'm here for my piano lesson. Are you Mrs. Finger... Finger...," I stammered.

"You mean, Mrs. Fingerschnitzel?" she asked.

"Yes, that's it!" I said, already liking this helpful woman and imagining how pleasant our piano lessons would be.

"No, you have the wrong house. She lives in number fourteen," she said and pointed to the end of the block.

"Thanks. Sorry for disturbing you," I said and walked away extremely disappointed.

"Didn't Mom say forty?" I asked Izzy.

"Guess not," she answered.

Izzy hopped ahead of me, like a carefree rabbit.

"Thirty-eight...thirty-six...thirty-four," she announced, pointing at every house.

I looked at her skipping ahead. *Maybe she should take lessons*, I thought.

"Twenty-two...twenty..."

That would curb her enthusiasm.

"Sixteen…fourteen…Oh, oh… Did that woman say fourteen?" she asked.

I looked at the house she was pointing at. It looked haunted! It looked like the house in the movie *Psycho*. I saw the movie at Maggie's a few months ago. We weren't supposed to watch it because we're too young and it's REALLY scary. But we did. We screamed our heads off. I missed most of the movie because I covered my eyes so much. All I remember is the way the house looked and it looked like this house! I also remember someone wearing a wig. But I could be confusing that with Grandma.

"This house looks haunted," Izzy read my mind.

I stood there, looking at the attic window, searching for the mother character from that horrifying movie. She lived in the attic, I think. Like I said, I missed most of the movie but this house looked oddly familiar.

"Did you hear what I said? This house looks haunted. I'm going home," Izzy announced and turned to go.

"No… Sss..Stay… Please," I stuttered.

"No way!" she protested and stomped her foot for emphasis.

We just stood there, glaring at each other and carefully glancing back at the Fingerschnitzel haunted house.

Maybe I can lie and tell Mom that Mrs. Fingerwhatever wasn't home. Or maybe I could say that she really was deaf. Or maybe…

Before I could finish my thought, the door flew open.

"You made it!" A silver-haired, tiny woman squealed and clapped her hands.

"I can't believe your mom let you walk here all alone," my new piano teacher said.

Me neither, I thought. But, out loud I said, "It's only 4 ½ blocks."

"You poor thing… And who's this little cutie?"

"I'm Isabelle but you can call me Izzy. I'm not your student. I'm just here to watch," she explained.

"So you must be Sofie. It's very nice to finally meet you," she extended her hand to shake mine. Her fingers looked totally fine. Not like any chicken schnitzel I ever saw sitting on a plate.

"Come on in ladies," she continued. "Let's go inside. It's too hot out here." She held the door for us and we stepped inside.

The first thing I noticed was the smell. The sweet smell of freshly made cookies hit my nose so abruptly that I forgot where I was for a second. I thought that I was at Grandma Martha's house in Oak Park.

Inside, the house was really bright and cheerful, nothing like the outside. I guess the saying, *don't judge a book by its cover,* would apply to this house. All the walls were painted a happy sunshine yellow. Even the sofa, the curtains, and the dining room seat cushions were yellow. Everything matched. I've never seen anything like it. *Grandma Ursula's house is a hodge-podge of colors and patterns. It can make you dizzy.*

Mrs. Fingerschnitzel looked like the inside of her house. She wore one color from head to toe. Lavender. She wasn't wearing a housedress either. She was wearing a fitted suit and make-up. She looked like she should be going out instead of staying in for a piano lesson. She may have looked as old as Grandma Ursula but that's all they had in common. And the most obvious difference between them? Mrs. Fingerschnitzel had no wig on her head. *Grandma throws on her wig in the morning and thinks she looks fabulous. She thinks it's some kind of a magic wand but it isn't. She should put a little more effort into her appearance.*

The piano was in a room that looked like a library. "Did you read all these books?" I asked.

"Yes," she replied.

"Wow," I said, pretty impressed.

"I don't have a TV, so - " she started to explain.

Izzy shot me a look of shock and disgust. *I have to agree with Izzy here. I can't imagine living without TV. (Thank God Grandma Ursula has...hmm...one, two...FOUR!)*

"Well let's get started. Isabelle, my dear, feel free..."

"It's Izzy," Izzy corrected my teacher.

"Oh, I'm terribly sorry. Izzy. Please feel free to read anything in here."

She's only 5, I thought, *she can't read.*

"I also have a doll house in the dining room you can play with. And there's a fresh batch of cookies in the kitchen," Mrs. Fingerschnitzel continued.

Well, as expected, Izzy stayed in the library with us for about 10 seconds before sneaking away into the kitchen.

"So, Sofie...Why don't we start with your favorite piece?" my teacher suggested.

"My favorite piece?" I repeated, surprised.

I don't have to do scales? I thought. I almost said that out loud but I caught myself just in time. *I don't want to give my new teacher any ideas. If she wants me to play songs I like, instead of those painful scales, then that's what I'll do.*

"Yes, your favorite piece," she answered, smiling.

I looked at the pretty pink lipstick she was wearing and noticed something weird. A piece of tape was hanging from her teeth.

Gross, I thought.

I must've made a face because she touched her mouth. "Oh, ooops...Sorry, I forgot I was still wearing my teeth-whitening strip," she said, blushing. She yanked it off and put it on top of the piano.

Gross, I thought again.

I played *Fur Elise*. It took a page and a half for me to forget about the whitening strip. I looked at her when I was done and noticed that she was wearing a hearing aid. That would explain Grandma's misunderstanding of Mrs. Fingerschnitzel's character.

"Bravo! Bravo!" my teacher exclaimed when I finished playing. I didn't think it was that great. I was a little rusty.

Izzy walked in, lured by the *bravos* and wild clapping. "What's going on?" she asked, chocolate all over her face, and a cookie in each hand.

"Oh no. No food allowed in this room," Mrs. Fingerschnitzel gasped. Izzy took a bite and left the room.

The half-hour lesson kind of flew by. "I'll see you at 3 o'clock next Tuesday?" she confirmed and opened the front door for us.

"Yes. And thank you," I answered politely.

"Thanks for the cookies," Izzy added.

"She's not deaf," Izzy announced as soon as Mrs. Fingerschnitzel closed the door behind us.

I guess Izzy didn't notice the hearing-aid. She's really not deaf if she's actually wearing it, I reassured myself.

"Shhh! What if she can still hear us?" I asked. "Did you eat the entire batch?" I added, unable to ignore the chocolate smears on her face.

"No, I left four on the tray," she began to explain.

"How generous," I rolled my eyes.

"And I brought one for you." She reached into her pocket and pulled out a sad looking cookie clump.

"Thanks." I almost got a little choked up. *My little sister barely thinks of anyone else, especially me.* I gave her a little hug. She looked up at me and smiled. She looked adorable, chocolate and all.

The first thing Grandma asked when we walked through the door was, "So, is she deaf?"

"Mrs. Fingerschnitzel? Deaf? No, I don't think so." I stretched the truth a bit.

"She's really nice," Izzy chimed in. "Her house looks really scary on the outside..."

"I'll say," Grandma interrupted.

"But inside it's really pretty. She looked really elegant too. And she's a great cook."

"How do you know?" Grandma interrupted again.

"How do I know what?" Izzy asked.

"How do you know that she's a great cook?"

"She gave me homemade cookies," Izzy answered.

"A whole batch," I added.

"Oh." Grandma frowned.

"So how was your piano lesson, sweetie?" Mom asked while making dinner.

"Good."

"Did you like your teacher?"

"Yeah. She's okay."

"Is she…uhm…do you think she has a hearing problem?"

"I don't think so." I neglected to mention the hearing-aid. *No need to worry Mom.*

"Good. So you'll go again next week?"

"I guess."

"I want to go too!" Izzy said, interrupting.

"You do? Why? You want to take lessons too?" Mom asked.

"No!" Izzy shook her head violently.

"She wants the cookies," I informed Mom.

"Cookies?" Mom asked.

"Yeah. She made a batch and Izzy ate them all."

"No I didn't. I left four and gave you one."

"How generous," I replied.

"How on earth are you going to eat dinner with all those cookies floating around in your tummy?" Mom asked, rubbing Izzy's stomach.

"Don't worry. I went to the bathroom twice. There's room." Izzy reassured Mom.

"Gross!" I said and pretended to vomit.

The following week, Izzy offered to accompany me to my piano lesson again.

How kind of you, I thought.

This time Mrs. Fingerschnitzel neglected to make a batch of cookies. She offered Izzy her library instead. Izzy looked at a couple of books and then went off to play with the doll house.

"I don't think I'm gonna come with you next week," she informed me when we left.

"Why?" I asked, even though I knew why.

"There are no pictures in her books... And she forgot to make cookies."

I knew my sister wouldn't last. But that was okay because my teacher was pretty nice. She was a little weird but that was okay. Today she had some of that tape *under* her eyes. Why would anyone put teeth-whitening strips under her eyes was beyond me. When I looked at her, I just pretended that I didn't see the tape. *As long as she doesn't make me do scales every time I come over, I couldn't care less where she sticks that tape. She can wrap it around her entire body and look like a mummy as far as I'm concerned. As long as she's nice, I'll tolerate her little weird habit.*

12

The Vase

Sometimes when I'm bored, I like to play tricks on Grandma. For example, I'll hide her keys, misplace a house slipper, wear her wig, or take her glasses hostage. The hostage situation is the most entertaining because she'll walk around the house like Frankenstein. With arms stretched out in front of her, Grandma roams around, threatening me (because she hears me chuckling nearby) and cursing the Almighty for making her nearly blind. Periodically she bumps into furniture. Sometimes things break.

And that's exactly what just happened.

Grandma collided with one of Mom's garage sale prized possessions —a porcelain *Limoges* vase that Mom fills with fresh flowers every chance she gets. Today the vase was empty but in pieces, seven big pieces to be exact, and Grandma was on the floor among the porcelain. The crash must've startled her and made her lose her balance.

"Are you okay, Grandma?" I was horrified. *This time I really did it.*

"This time you really did it!" Grandma read my mind. "Look at your mom's vase! She's going to be really upset," she added, rubbing her hip. She's been limping a little the last couple of days.

Forget how mad Mom might be, when Dad finds out that I made Grandma a cripple, he'll kill me, or at least ground me for life. "Are you okay, Grandma?" I asked, worried about *her* hip and my future.

"I'm fine. My hip's just acting up a bit. Your silly little game certainly didn't help matters," she snapped back at me and squinted her eyes for emphasis.

There was no need for Grandma to emphasize the gravity of this situation. I was pretty terrified. "What are we going to do?" I asked, thinking about the broken vase.

"I know what I will do. I will tell your parents that you are a terror and should be punished," Grandma began to say.

"No! Please don't. I'll never hide your glasses again. I promise!"

"You got that right."

"I'll clean your room," I offered.

She thought about it for a moment. "Go on."

"And…make you breakfast for a week?" I added.

"You already do that," she pointed out.

"Right. I'll make lunch for a week."

"That's an interesting idea," she smiled (or was it a smirk?) and gave me her hand. "Help me up, would you?"

"So. It's a deal?"

"Yep. I'll keep quiet about your little shenanigans and you'll cook lunch. Forget about cleaning my room. I don't want you roaming around in there."

"So what about the vase?" I suddenly remembered the evidence laying on the floor in seven pieces.

"The vase is your problem," she snapped back at me. "I'll get you some glue," she said and limped away rubbing her hip.

The vase looked like a 3-D puzzle. *I can do this with my eyes closed*, I predicted. I considered myself an expert at puzzles. But just in case, I kept my eyes open.

The directions on the bottle of glue were pretty straightforward. With the exception of a tiny detail, a detail involving water, I was convinced the instructions would be fully implemented. *As long as Mom doesn't decide to put fresh flowers in the vase for the next forty-eight hours, everything will be fine.*

Just then, I heard a car door slam.

"Mom's back!" I announced in horror. "And she bought flowers!" I don't know who I said this to, because no one was in the kitchen at this point.

But Grandma must have heard me from the other room because she limped into the kitchen and said, "Oh, your mom bought a bouquet of roses. How nice."

"What should I do?" I asked Grandma.

Before Grandma could answer, Mom walked into the kitchen and said, "Sofie, can you please help me with the groceries? Are you okay? You look pale." She put the flowers next to the sink and touched my forehead.

I couldn't speak. Grandma, on the other hand, could and said, "Anne, I need to borrow your *Limoges* vase."

"But I just bought flowers - " Mom tried to explain.

I held my breath.

"I just need it for tonight. Sally and Edith are coming over for a game of rummy. I want to liven up the table a bit. It's the prettiest vase we have. And if we put flowers in it, I won't be able to see their faces and study their moves," Grandma explained and then she added, "Sally and Edith can be pretty sneaky."

I couldn't believe Grandma just came up with that. She picked up the patched up vase, gave me a *you-owe-me* look, and walked out of the room.

Luckily, Mom doesn't argue with her mother-in-law. She sighed and went looking for another vase.

I started breathing again. I followed Grandma into the family room and said, "Grandma, I'm really sorry I played that trick on you and that you got hurt."

"I hope you learned your lesson. And about my hip, listen, it's been bothering me for a while now. You just sped up the inevitable."

"What's that?" I asked.

"I have to call the doctor…. Oh, and now I have to call Sally and Edith too."

"Why?"

"To tell them to come over for a game of rummy," she answered.

"You mean you made it all up?" I asked.

She didn't answer. She just smiled.

The next day, to my horror, Mom filled the *Limoges* vase with water and put the roses in it. *It hasn't been forty-eight hours!* But I couldn't tell her that.

Grandma walked in, saw Mom, and gasped. We stared at the vase.

Nothing.

Grandma shrugged.

We're safe, I predicted.

I was wrong. Water started gushing out from the various cracks. The vase looked like the Buckingham Fountain on Lake Shore Drive.

I lunged at it. Grandma hopped over like a gazelle. We both tried to grab it but we knocked it over instead. It fell apart, into seven pieces.

"Oh, no! It broke again!" Mom exclaimed, as she walked in the room.

"Again?" Grandma and I asked simultaneously.

"I knocked it over a few days ago," Mom explained.

Hmm. Maybe I don't have to confess after all, I thought.

Grandma read my mind and gave me a disapproving look.

"Mom," I started to say.

"Yes?"

"I have something to tell you…"

13

THE SURPRISE VISIT

"**W**ho's that?" I asked and pointed at the suspicious looking silhouette in the dimly-lit family room. It was a rainy, gloomy, warm July evening.

"Where?" Grandma asked and peered into the room carefully. She turned the lights on and said, "Oh, you mean my other head?"

She decided to buy another Styrofoam head so she wouldn't have to schlep upstairs every time she wanted her wig. Actually, I've been doing the schlepping since she hurt her hip. It was part of my punishment, I'm sure.

Grandma decided to keep her new Styrofoam acquisition in the pantry. She put the wig on the Styrofoam and arranged it carefully, as though it was on her own head. I didn't think it was such a good idea (keeping it in the pantry) and, judging by Mom's piercing scream when she opened the pantry, neither did Mom. But it was Grandma's house after all, so Mom had to tread lightly.

"Hmm," Mom cleared her throat. "Ursula, do you think it might be unsanitary to keep this wig in the pantry, so close to food?"

"Nonsense," Grandma replied, using her favorite word in the English language. "Besides, I'm not trying to showcase this thing." And then she added, "It might scare visitors if it's out in the open."

But it's okay to terrify us with these decapitations, I wondered, taking Mom's side.

"If you think it's dangerously close to food then take some of it out. There's too much food in the pantry anyway." And like a hairdresser might do with a real person, Grandma stepped in front of the fake head and fluffed up the heap of fake hair. "There," she said, looking satisfied. "That's better."

I don't know what she was looking at, but the wig looked identical pre- and post- fluffing. If there was any improvement, I didn't see it.

She closed the pantry door carefully, so as not to disturb the perfectly-coiffed wig. Then she looked at us and said, "Don't slam this door," as if that's what we've been doing all this time —slamming doors.

Mom and I looked at each other and nodded in agreement. *When it comes to Grandma's wig, it's better to just agree.*

The next morning Izzy flew through the kitchen (she can never just walk) and announced, "Andrew's back from camp!"

"So?" I said, as nonchalantly as possible.

"Aren't you interested?" she stopped in her tracks and looked at me real close.

"No." I lied. *I wonder if he still remembers the two embarrassing wig incidents or the underwear nightmare? Probably.*

"I wonder if he still remembers you running in the street in your underwear?" she asked. "Probably," she answered her own question, laughing.

Ungrateful brat! I thought. *I was trying to save your life! Next time you're on your own.*

"Girls," Mom walked into the kitchen and announced, "I have great news!"

"What is it?" Izzy and I blurted out in unison.

"Grandma Martha is coming tomorrow," she said, smiling.

"Hurray!" Izzy jumped up and down.

"Are you serious?" I was thrilled.

"I take it you told the girls?" Dad walked into the kitchen.

"Grandma's coming!" Izzy announced.

"I know, sweetheart," he said and filled up two cups of coffee, one for him and one for Grandma Ursula. She wasn't up to walking down the stairs yet, even with her cane.

"Girls, you have to help me clean the house today. There's so much to do…. I don't know where she'll sleep…."

"Sofie can sleep on the couch," Izzy offered. "And Grandma Martha can sleep in Sofie's bed.

How nice of you to offer my bed, I thought. "No way! That couch is awful," I protested. " I fell asleep on it once and when I got up I couldn't walk."

"You're right, we'll think of something," Mom agreed.

"Izzy can sleep with you and Dad. And Grandma Martha can sleep in Izzy's bed," I offered, hoping to get back at Izzy and her selfish plan to get Grandma all to herself and evict me from my own room.

"You and Grandma will be roommates?" she asked, shaking her head. "I don't think so!"

"It's a better idea than the one *you* came up with," I nodded my head for emphasis.

"No!" Izzy shook her head.

"That's enough, both of you. Thanks for your suggestions but I'll decide who's going to sleep where…. Now who wants to vacuum?" she asked, looking for volunteers.

Dad raised his hand.

I cleaned the kitchen, Mom cleaned the bathrooms and Izzy cleaned up all her toys. Her job was the easiest, as usual.

While Dad was vacuuming, Grandma Ursula apparently yelled for help. She had to go to the bathroom and needed help getting up from her bed because she couldn't reach her cane. Well, nobody heard her because of all the noise Dad was making. So she had a little accident. She spent the next hour complaining about us ignoring her. Dad couldn't take it anymore, so he got into his car and drove off. He came back a few minutes later with a brown paper bag.

"Here," he said and handed the bag to Grandma.

"What is it?" she asked, with a little twinkle in her eye. "A present?" She looked inside and frowned, "A whistle?"

"Yep," Dad answered. "If you need anything, use it."

Grandma took it out of the bag and said, "Thank you." She blew the whistle right in Dad's ear, "Just making sure it works."

I feel bad admitting this, but it's kind of good that Grandma Ursula hurt her hip. I don't wish her harm or anything, but that's why Grandma Martha is coming. She's going to help watch us until Grandma Ursula is better.

After our Sunday brunch, Izzy ran into the kitchen and announced, "She's here! She's here!"

We raced outside.

"My angels," Grandma Martha cried.

"We missed you so much," I told her and gave her a giant hug. She smelled like apple pie, of course.

Sometimes when I really missed Grandma Martha, I would go to a local bakery just for the smell. The first time I did that, I stood in the middle of the bakery, innocently inhaling. But the purple-haired girl behind the counter leered at me through her thick, black eye-liner as though I was weird. *You're the one with purple hair*, I thought. As I stood there, I realized that I should probably buy something but I didn't have any money. *You can't just go to a bakery and take deep breaths*, I told myself. That's why the purple-haired girl was staring at me. So the next time I felt an urge for the smell, I snuck into Grandma Ursula's room, located her purse, and took some change. No bills, just coins. *Nobody cares about coins.* So I wasn't really stealing. Besides, it wasn't my fault Grandma Ursula didn't bake. Back at the bakery, I took my time deciding —smelling the brownies, the cherry pies, the banana bread —and pretended I couldn't make up my mind. When the purple-haired girl glared at me suspiciously, I jiggled the stolen coins in my pocket to reassure her that I was there to make a purchase.

"Hi Mom. Thank you for coming on such a short notice," my mom said and kissed Grandma Martha.

"We really appreciate it," my dad added.

"I'm thrilled to see you all," she said, wiping her tears. "Let me look at you girls. You're getting so big Izzy…. And Sofie, are you as tall as me?" she asked, covering her mouth in shock.

"Almost," I noticed that she was right.

"Mom, you lost weight," Mom said, inspecting Grandma.

"A little bit," she answered.

"Are you OK?" Mom asked.

"I'm great. Where's Ursula?"

"She's in her room," Dad answered.

"Let me go in and say hello," she said and walked into the house.

"How long is Grandma staying?" Izzy asked.

"Two weeks. Just until my classes end. Then I'll stay home if Grandma Ursula needs me," Mom answered.

"Just two weeks?" I asked, disappointed. *We've been gone so long and she's only staying two weeks?*

"She has to get back home," Mom explained.

"Why?" I asked.

"I don't know, sweetheart. She didn't say."

That's weird, I thought. *Whenever we talked on the phone, she always said how much she missed us. And now that she's here, she can only stay two weeks? I must investigate.*

14

A SHOCKING UPDATE

*T*hat night, when everyone was in bed, I asked Grandma, "How come you're only staying two weeks?"

I expected her to say that she'll stay longer but instead she said, "I have to get back, sweetie."

To what? I thought. *She doesn't have a job.*

I flipped over onto my stomach and dug my elbows into the soft mattress so I could think better. I looked at Grandma and asked, "Why?"

"It's been a long day, Sofie. I'm really tired from the drive. Let's get some sleep. We can talk tomorrow. Okay?"

I had no choice but to agree. "Okay," I answered, disappointed.

The next day, I cornered Grandma Martha after lunch.

"Can you please tell me why you only want to stay two weeks?" I persisted.

"I can't stay longer," she replied.

"Why?" I asked. My patience was running low.

"Because I have to get back," she answered.

This back and forth - questions but no answers - went on for a few more rounds until I got dizzy but I persisted anyway. My determination paid off because Grandma began to crack.

"Well, you have to promise to let *me* tell your mom…," she began her confession.

"I promise," I assured her and crossed my heart to show her I really meant it.

"You promise what?" Izzy flew into the living room and plopped down on the couch. *My sister has the worst timing.* "What are you ladies gossiping about?" she asked, smiling.

"Why don't you go play with your friends?" I said and pointed at the front door to show her the way.

"No!" she answered and crossed her arms.

My interrogation will have to wait, I thought.

When everyone was finally in bed, I brought up the subject again.

"Boy, you sure are persistent, Sofia," she said and looked at me for a second. "You have to promise to let *me* tell your mom," she whispered.

"Of course. I promise."

Grandma's insistence on secrecy started to worry me. *What if she's sick?* I wondered. *I love my grandma. She's one of my favorite people. I want her to live forever, and if not forever then at least for a very long time, at least until I get married. What if she has cancer? Or a bad case of diabetes? Maybe she needs a transplant and wants one of my organs. I wonder which one? What do I have two of? I could spare a lung. She could have one of my kidneys. Do I have two livers? I should really pay more attention in school.*

"I have a giant secret," she whispered and leaned in closer to my face. She was smiling.

"What is it?" I leaned toward her, filled with hope. *It can't be bad news if she's smiling*, I predicted with relief.

"Well, how can I put this? Uhm, your parents don't know yet. And I don't know how to tell them either. But I have to before I leave here."

"What is it?" I interrupted impatiently.

"Oh, I'll just come out with it fast, I suppose. That's really the only way - "

"Grandma!" I was getting really annoyed.

"Well, what? This is not easy for me."

"How do you think I feel?"

"What?"

"I'm dying to know your secret. I promise I won't tell anyone. Just tell me already!"

"I have a gentleman friend," she said, staring right into my eyes.

"A…A what?" I stammered.

"A companion," she said, as if to clarify.

"Huh?"

"A friend who's a man."

"You mean a boyfriend?" I asked, shocked.

"I guess you can call him that," she chuckled.

"At your age?" I blurted out. "I mean, no offense. But, at *your* age?" I whispered.

The whole idea just grossed me out. *I mean, I don't even have a boyfriend. What's wrong with this world? I asked myself. I'm ten and there's no boyfriend in sight. But Grandma? She's like a hundred years old. OK, not a hundred. She's sixty-one, but still. She should act her age. What is she going to do with this boyfriend? She's going to walk around Oak Park and hold hands? That's just ridiculous. Oh, no! She's going to kiss him. Gross! Grandma's going to kiss some old smelly man. What would Grandpa say about that? If he was still alive, he'd tell her that she was crazy.*

When Grandma said she had a secret, I thought it was going to be a good one. *This is a total nightmare, I concluded. My grandma's going to be running around Oak Park with her ancient boyfriend.*

What if some of my old friends see her? I never thought I'd say this, but THANK GOD we moved. This news gave me a giant headache.

"Are you okay, Sofie?" she asked.

Just wait 'til Mom finds out, I looked at my unsuspecting grandma. *She'll set you straight! She'll tell you that you're completely crazy. She'll make you break up with this guy and she'll tell you to act your age!*

"Sofie?"

"Huh?"

"Are you okay?"

"I'm really tired."

"You're right, it's late. Let's get some sleep," she said and kissed my forehead. Two seconds later, she was out.

And me? I was still leaning in toward her pillow. I was waiting for her to wake up and tell me that she made it all up. Instead, she was snoring. *How can she sleep at a time like this?* I wondered.

15

ANOTHER REVELATION

"Are you okay, Sofie?" Mom touched my forehead when I walked into the kitchen the following morning.

"Yeah, I'm just a little tired." That was a major understatement. I didn't sleep all night. I could barely walk.

I glanced over at my grandmas who were huddled together at the kitchen table. They were sitting ten inches apart and were looking at each other. Their mouths were conveniently hidden behind their coffee mugs so I couldn't tell what they were whispering. It looked like they were cooking up some conspiracy.

Grandma Martha looked at me, moved her mug away from her face, and smiled. I gave her a *don't-worry-I-won't-say-a-word* look and plopped down in a chair next to her.

"Would you like me to make you a waffle, Sofie?" she asked.

A bribe? Nice touch, Grandma, I thought.

Before I could answer, Grandma was up fetching all the ingredients. The thought of waffles almost made me forgive her. Almost.

I'll be nice to you Grandma because your news is not going to go over well with the rest of the family. They're not as open-minded and understanding as me.

After breakfast, I decided to go to the library and get a book.

"Can you recommend a book without any grandma characters?" I asked the librarian.

"No grandmas?" the librarian asked and tilted her head.

"Yep," I answered firmly. I was not about to explain myself to the nosey librarian. *It's none of her business if I'm a little annoyed with my grandma right now.*

"Well, I think we can find something for you," she replied quickly and walked away.

She came back with a stack of eight or ten books. "I found a few books. If you'd like to have a look and pick which ones look interesting."

"I'll take them all," I said.

"Well, you can only check out five," she explained.

"Okay." I counted five books from the top of the stack without even looking at the titles. "I'll take these," I said, unenthusiastically.

"Really? Oh, okay," she said. She looked a little disappointed. What did she want?

Should I be jumping up and down because I'm checking out five books? Big deal! She should be glad that I'm not hiding behind the library and smoking a cigarette instead. She should look on the bright side. I'M READING.

I was so distracted by Grandma's crazy news last night that I totally passed up our house on my way back from the library.

"That's Andrew's house," Izzy announced from our porch.

I looked up and, sure enough, I was standing in front of his house. All of a sudden, the books felt really heavy and I dropped them.

"Why are you throwing books on the ground?" Izzy asked and ran toward me.

"They fell," I answered.

"Guess what?" Izzy has a way of changing the subject just like that.

"What?" I asked, uninterested.

"Mom and Grandma threw me out of the house."

"What?" I asked, a little intrigued.

"Yep."

"Why?"

"Grandma wanted to talk to Mom about something."

"Did Mom get mad and holler at Grandma?" I asked, nodding my head.

"No."

"No?"

"Well, I don't know. I tried listening through the door but I couldn't hear them at all. Why would Mom get mad at Grandma?"

"You'll see," I warned my clueless sister.

Just then, the door flew open and Grandma Ursula stood in the middle of it. "Great news! Come in girls."

We came into the kitchen and saw Mom and Grandma Martha hugging. Mom looked at us and said, "Your Grandma is getting married!"

I looked at Grandma Ursula and she shook her head, "Oh, no, no. Not me. Your other grandma," she pointed at Grandma Martha.

Grandma Martha was beaming.

"Married?" I managed to say. "Married?" I repeated.

"Married?" Izzy echoed my shock.

"Married?" I asked again, unable to think of anything else to say.

"What's wrong with you two?" Grandma Ursula asked, shaking her head. "Give your grandma a big kiss and tell her *congratulations*."

"Congratulations Grandma," Izzy said and gave her a big kiss. "But aren't you too old to get married?"

I love it when my little sister asks exactly what I'd love to ask but am too scared to. I waited for an answer to this excellent question. Instead, they all just laughed.

"Congratulations Grandma," I said, trying to smile. Then I started to think. How did the companion/boyfriend from last night's conversation become a fiancé this afternoon? Did she lie to me last night? Did she *forget* to mention that she was already engaged? She called him a companion. *I can't believe it*!

"So how and *when* did he propose? It must've been really romantic." I decided to investigate.

"He called me this morning and asked me," she explained, smiling.

"He proposed on the *phone*?" I asked, totally shocked. This guy sounded like a total loser. I always thought that Grandma Martha was a sensible woman. Guess not! She said 'yes' to a guy who proposed on the phone? And what made everything worse was that no one in the room thought that there was something wrong with this picture. *Wait 'til Dad hears about this*, I predicted.

"That's great news!" Dad exclaimed as soon as all the other overly excited women let him talk.

So much for a rational response to Grandma Martha's news, I thought. *My whole family is crazy.*

Rather than fret and worry about Grandma's ridiculous decision to marry a man who proposed on the phone, I decided to enjoy her company and her delicious food. And soon the two weeks were over. Her departure was as sudden as her arrival. We all cried as we said our good-byes, well, everyone except Grandma Ursula. She was smiling. She stood on her front porch in her pink housedress and waved her cane. Dust flew up from the gravel driveway as Grandma Martha sped away from us.

16

GOOD NEWS

During Grandma Martha's brief visit, I totally forgot about Andrew. So you can imagine my shock when I heard, "Hey, Sofia, are you gonna go to the block party next Sunday?"

"The what?" I asked, startled.

"The block party. We always have one a couple of weeks before school starts," he explained.

"Grandma didn't tell me - "

"Well, she usually just sits on her porch and someone gets her a plate of food - "

"Oh." I imagined Grandma sitting on her porch all by herself and kind of felt sorry for her.

"So, will you?"

"Will I what?" I asked, absentmindedly.

"Will you be here?"

"I guess so. We're not going anywhere."

"Good. Some kids from school will be there, kids who'll be in your class."

"How do you know what grade I'll be in?" I asked, thrilled that Andrew has asked about me.

"Izzy told me. She talks about you a lot," he said.

I bet she does, I thought.

That night, Mom asked me if I want Maggie to come for a visit.

"Are you kidding?" I squealed. "Yes!"

"That's not fair," Izzy interrupted.

"Who would you like to invite here, Izzy?" Mom asked.

"I don't know," Izzy said and shrugged.

"Well, when you think of someone, let me know," Mom suggested and kissed Izzy on the forehead.

"Can Maggie stay for a week?" I asked.

"Sure, I don't see why not," Mom answered.

I almost tripped over Grandma, trying to get to the phone.

Maggie's little brother, Jack, answered the phone.

"I have to talk to your sister," I announced quickly.

"Who's this?" he asked.

"It's Sofie, hurry up!" I said.

"I can't wait to get a cell phone." I heard Maggie say to Jack.

"You're getting a cell phone?" I asked, a little jealous.

"Sofie, is that you?" Maggie asked, ignoring my question.

"Yes. Guess what?" I asked.

"No. You guess what!" she said.

"Okay. What?" I asked.

"My mom said I can come over for a week!"

"I know. My mom just told me," I said.

"I can't wait," Maggie squealed happily.

"This is gonna be awesome," I predicted.

17

WHAT?

"What's wrong with you?" Grandma Ursula asked.

I was staring at my breakfast. "It won't be good cold," she continued and pointed at my French toast with her fork.

"I know," I said, unconcerned. I should've been thrilled because Maggie was coming but I was in a major funk.

She put my toast on her plate and looked at me. "Do you plan on frowning all day?"

I looked at her but did not answer.

"I know. You miss your grandma. Not me, of course," she explained with a little smirk, "your *other* grandma."

I smiled because this statement was true and also because Grandma Ursula had a knack for guessing what I thought.

"Well, are you going to talk or do I have to whack you with my cane to make you talk," she asked, raising her cane jokingly.

"No, please don't beat me Grandma!" I pretended to cry.

"Seriously, what's wrong? I have a feeling that it's not just your grandma's departure that's making you sad," she guessed correctly and gave me a serious look.

I decided to just come out with it. "Well, ever since I found out that we were moving in with you, and not Grandma Martha, I was wondering why," I said. What I really wanted to ask was, *why didn't we move in with my favorite grandma?* But I didn't dare say *that* out loud. That would be really rude.

"You mean why didn't you move in with your favorite grandma?" she read my mind, again.

"Why move all the way here, to a different state?" I asked, ignoring her question.

"Why change schools? Why not stay in Oak Park and move in with Grandma Martha? I mean I know why we couldn't stay in *our* house. But why couldn't we move in with the Grandma who was just a few blocks away? I don't get it!"

"Why move in with me?" she asked.

"No offense," I reassured her.

"None taken. It's complicated, Sofia. But I suppose you'll just waste time, moping around the house and making me miserable, until someone finally explains everything to you."

"Mom told me that the bank took our house because we couldn't make the payments," I explained.

"Yes, that was bad news," she said and nodded her head.

"What I don't get is why didn't Grandma Martha insist that we move in with her? Or why didn't my parents ask if we could live with her?"

"They did."

"What? They asked her?" I almost fell off my chair in shock.

"Yes. They wanted to stay in Oak Park," she said and cleared her throat. "But your grandma didn't think it was a good idea."

"Huh?" I couldn't believe it. All this time, I thought my parents never bothered to ask Grandma Martha. They asked? And she said no? Unbelievable! I thought she loved us. She always cooked for us. She made our Halloween costumes. She played games with us. She loved our visits! Didn't she?

"How could she?" I blurted out.

"She had her reasons, good reasons," Grandma said and moved her plate aside.

I started sniffling.

"Sofie, your grandma loves you and Izzy more than anything in this world," she said and clasped her hands together. "First, the obvious and practical reason, her house is really small. You would all get on each other's nerves soon. Believe me, I grew up in a tiny house. I know. I *still* don't talk to my sister," she paused and frowned a little. "Second, your clever grandma thought that I should have the opportunity to enjoy you girls for a few years too. I mean how many times a year did I see you? Once? Twice? Maybe three times?" She took a deep breath. "You know, I too love you more than anything in this world. I may not show it that much, not being a big hugger and all. But I'm so glad you're here. You don't realize how lonely you are until you're not lonely anymore." Her eyes got a little watery. She scratched her wig-less head. "I wish you didn't try to set my house on fire," she joked. "But I'm glad things worked out the way they did." She smiled at me.

Grandma Ursula saved us from being homeless? I looked at her soft, sad, baby-fine gray hair. This whole summer I thought we were just a temporary nuisance to her. *Maybe we're not a nuisance after all.* I hugged her. She held me really tight. The last time I hugged her was when we arrived. *I should do this more often*, I thought.

Grandma got up to turn up the volume on the TV. I didn't realize it was on. It was some cooking show, of course. *For someone who doesn't like to cook, she sure loves to watch other people do it. For her, cooking is what my dad would call, a spectator sport.*

"Grandma, why do you love watching these cooking shows?" I asked.

"I don't know. It's a habit, I guess."

"Like your wig is a habit?"

"Leave my wig out of it," she paused and gave me a stern look. "Cooking is like a story."

"A story?" I was confused. I imagined a carrot talking to a celery stick and shook my head at the impossibility.

"Yes, a story. It has a beginning, a middle, and an end. It's predictable. You chop up some meat and vegetables, cook them, and throw them on a plate," she explained. I must've still looked confused because she added, "Or maybe I'm just hoping that these chefs' love of cooking will rub off on me."

"Has it?"

"Not yet," she chuckled. "But I'm patient."

18

MAGGIE

*T*his past week, I finally had something good to look forward to this summer! Maggie.

I cleaned up our room and threw down a sleeping bag for Izzy who, by the way, wasn't thrilled to be demoted to the bedroom floor. Mom gave Izzy a choice: sleep in their bed or join us for a week-long slumber party. She chose the slumber party. She just didn't anticipate she'd end up on the floor. Surprisingly, Izzy didn't complain. She likes Maggie.

While I was busy cleaning our room, Izzy was glued to the living room window. You'd think Maggie was her friend. "She's here! She's here!" Izzy announced.

I started to run down the stairs when Grandma called from the front door, "Sofia, grab my wig, would you?"

I ran into her room and yanked the wig off the unsuspecting Styrofoam head. It wobbled a bit, just like Mom's "Dwight" wobble head does (that's "Dwight" from the *Office* - Mom's favorite show).

I flew down the stairs, skipping two or three steps at a time. It's a miracle I didn't kill myself. I gave Grandma her wig.

"How do I look?" she asked, arranging her wig.

"Great," I said and I wasn't even lying. Grandma was wearing the same wig and the same pink housedress but she looked good. She just seemed different. I couldn't explain why but I didn't have time to figure it out because Maggie was here.

I ran up to Maggie. We collided and hugged.

Maggie's mom walked up to Grandma and said, "Hi, I'm Lauren, Maggie's mom."

"It's nice to meet you. I'm Ursula. Anne couldn't be here. She has a class - " Grandma started to say.

"I know. She told me. Thank you so much for letting Maggie stay."

"Oh, don't mention it. Are you hungry?" Grandma asked, even though she didn't cook anything.

"Oh, no, no, no. Thank you."

I wondered if she knew about Grandma's cabbage soup. Maybe Maggie told her about it.

"I have to get back," she said and then looked at Maggie. "Now, Maggie, you behave. Do you hear me?"

"Yes, Mom." They hugged and kissed and her mom drove away.

"So what are we going to do?" Izzy asked hopefully.

"What do you mean *we*?" I asked. "Why don't you go play with your neighbor friend. What's her name?"

"Ellie."

"Yeah, go play with Ellie," I suggested.

"She's not home," Izzy said and stomped her foot.

"Too bad," I replied.

"Come with me," Grandma interrupted and took Izzy's hand.

Over the next couple of days Maggie and I did what we'd do in Oak Park in the summertime. We went out for ice cream. We went to the pool and the park. Sometimes we just walked around aimlessly. We also did something we would *not* do in Oak Park, we spied on Andrew.

"He's gorgeous," Maggie admitted, her eyes bulging.

"I know," I agreed proudly, as though *I* had something to do with it.

"Doesn't he have a girlfriend?" she asked.

"I don't know. It doesn't seem like it. I'd see her around, wouldn't I? He does have a lot of friends, though."

"That means he's nice. That's good," she said.

"Yeah… But he must think I'm a freak," I said.

"I bet he forgot all about the wig…. And the underwear," she giggled.

"I doubt it." I sighed.

"Let's go out and talk to him," she suggested.

"No! Are you crazy?" I gasped.

"Well, I'm going," she said and started to walk away.

"Wait…. I'm coming. Let me change first." I ran to my closet. Maggie joined me.

"I don't know what to wear."

"Wear this," she said and pulled out the exact outfit I wore on that fateful day two months ago; the day that marked me as a freak; the underwear incident day.

"No way, are you crazy?"

"No, just the opposite. Listen, if you wear the same outfit you wore on that day, you're going to replace *that* embarrassing memory in his head with a *new* one, a positive one."

"Huh?" I was confused.

"You have to look the same. You're going to replace that embarrassing memory with a new memory, a day where Sofia appears to be normal and isn't running around the neighborhood in her purple underwear."

"Where did you come up with such a crazy idea?" I asked.

"I saw it in a movie," she replied.

"I don't know." I wasn't convinced.

"Sofia, just do it!" She looked so sure that I obeyed. I dug up my diamond-studded flip-flops to complete my outfit and off we went.

"Hey, Sofia!" Andrew called from his garage. He was arranging some recycling bins.

"Oh, hi Andrew," I said, acting surprised to see him. "This is Maggie, my best friend. She's visiting from Oak Park."

"Hi," he said and smiled.

"Hi," Maggie replied and blushed.

"Will you come to the block party tomorrow?" he asked, looking at me.

"Oh, I almost forgot," I lied. I'd been thinking about it ever since he mentioned it. I created various romantic scenarios in which pretty much the same thing happened at the end - Andrew took me in his arms and kissed me on the mouth.

"So are you?"

"What? Oh, I guess. We'll probably be there. We're not going anywhere." I tried to kick a pebble with my flip-flop. Instead, the stupid rock got stuck between my big toe *and* the flip-flop. I stood on my heel and wiggled my foot to get the rock out. It wasn't working.

"Are you okay?" he asked, looking at my foot.

"Yeah," I said, embarrassed.

"I guess I'll see you then," he said and then turned to Maggie. "See you later." He hopped on his bike and pedaled away.

"OMG! He's gorgeous up close," Maggie blurted out when he was gone.

"Is that why you were so quiet?" I asked.

"Yeah…I…I…couldn't…I didn't know what to say," she stammered.

"I told you. He should be on TV, *not* in Stevens Point."

"Yeah, you're so lucky…" she said.

"Why?" I interrupted.

"…to be living next to him."

I never thought of this town as being a lucky place to live.

19

The BBQ

*T*he next morning Maggie and I snuck into the kitchen so we could surprise everyone and make a big brunch but Grandma was already there. She was sitting at the table, drinking coffee from her Snoopy mug. She had a notebook in her other hand and was fanning her face.

It was a hot August morning. The kitchen was even more stuffy than the upstairs. Luckily, Grandma had ceiling fans in all the upstairs bedrooms but I can't say they helped that much. Downstairs, she just had a couple of fans that you could move from room to room. She had both of them in the kitchen today and they were both aimed at her. Her housedress was flapping in the wind. *I don't know how Grandma lasted this long without air-conditioning.*

"Hi girls," she raised her cup.

"Hi. We're going to make some eggs, bacon, and - " I started to say.

"Oh, don't bother," she took a sip.

Is Grandma going to cook? I wondered. *No, that's crazy.*

"There they are," she said and pointed out the open window.

"Who?" I asked.

"The neighbors. Don't you hear them? The squeaky wheels?" And then she added, whispering, "It's the barbeque."

Sure enough, people from three or four different houses were pulling their grills out on the sidewalk. Andrew was one of them. He looked so strong.

I remembered that the barbeque was today. I just didn't expect it to start first thing in the morning. That's not how we did it in Oak Park. Usually, people started gathering in the afternoon and the block party would go on into the night. At this rate, this barbeque will be over before noon. *That's pretty lame. That's Stevens Point for you.*

Grandma got up and headed for the pantry. She opened it and grabbed her wig. She placed it on her head, fluffed it up a little, glanced at herself in the microwave door, and went out on the front porch. We followed. She sat on her porch swing and repeated, "It's the barbeque."

Maggie and I nodded in agreement. We stood next to Grandma and watched the commotion. After the grills were all set up, more people came out on the street, carrying tables and lawn chairs.

I realized that we were still in our pajamas. I looked at Maggie and pointed at her and myself. She understood immediately and nodded. We snuck back into the house. *I don't think Grandma noticed our departure.* She was *that* mesmerized by the promise of food.

We met Izzy on the staircase. She flew by, already dressed, announcing, "It's the barbeque! Hurry up and get dressed."

"I know," I answered. "But it's not ready yet. They're still setting up." I don't think she heard me though because she was out the door before I finished talking.

Maggie and I got dressed pretty fast, considering Andrew was in the picture. Maggie picked out a couple of random outfits, nothing extraordinary, and I just obeyed.

When we came back out, Grandma was talking to some neighbor I've never met on our porch. She waved her hand and said, "Oh, that's how it goes." They both laughed.

I looked around for Izzy and saw her standing next to a giant platter of cookies. "Take it easy with those," I warned her, remembering what she did at the Fingerschnitzel house.

"Mind your own business," she snapped back rudely.

"Hey, do you want to play a game?" Maggie asked Izzy.

"Sure. What?" she asked. Only Izzy would agree first and then ask for specifics. Maggie took her hand and they ran into our garage to get something.

I looked around for Andrew. I saw him talking to a group of kids. When he noticed me, he said something to the group and then walked over to where I was standing. Two girls from Andrew's entourage, dressed in cut-offs and blue hoodies, followed him.

"This is Abby and Sarah," he said. "And this is Sofia, the fastest sprinter in Stevens Point."

That was not necessary, I thought.

"Hi," I said to the girls. I couldn't figure out if they were twins or what. They kind of looked the same —skinny, my height, and long brown straight hair —and were wearing identical clothes.

"Hi. We're gonna be in the same class together," Sarah informed me. "Miss Lynch's class."

"She's pretty nice," Abby chimed in.

"She's better than Miss Owen, the other fifth grade teacher," Sarah added.

"Oh, that's good," I replied. I realized that I hadn't once thought about the new school year during this crazy summer.

"Well, see you next week," Sarah said and walked back to the group. Abby followed.

I could already tell which one of them was the leader and which one was the follower. Sarah was the leader. She did most of the talking. I started to wonder and worry what all the other girls in my class will be like. Like I said before, I hadn't thought about school once during this entire chaotic summer. I was a little worried. *What if all the girls are really mean and bossy? Or what if they are wimpy and uninteresting? Who will I be friends with? What if - ?*

"So, when's Maggie going back?" Andrew interrupted my thoughts.

"Tomorrow," I answered, realizing how quickly the week flew by. I looked over at Maggie playing hopscotch with Izzy. *I won't be the only one who'll miss Maggie,* I predicted.

"Hey, Andrew, Mom needs your help," his little sister called from their front lawn.

"I gotta go," he said and walked away.

I went up to Grandma, who was sitting alone now, and asked, "Do you want me to get you a plate of food?"

"Yes, would you?" she asked.

"Grandma, weren't we supposed to make something too? You know, contribute some food?" I asked, concerned.

"Well, I usually don't. I don't think they expect a senior citizen to be cooking up a storm for this barbeque." She thought for a moment and added, "Why don't you go into the pantry and see if you can find some chips."

I went into the pantry and was greeted by Grandma's Styrofoam head. It startled me a bit. I still wasn't used to it sitting in the middle of the pantry. And as if *that* wasn't enough, a couple of weeks ago, Izzy decided to decorate the Styrofoam head. She must've been bored. No big surprise in Stevens Point. She decided to give the Styrofoam head a make-over. *She's no expert, obviously, so the thing looks pretty ghastly. The now green-eyed head has thick purple eye-liner and pink eye-shadow.* Izzy also applied some rouge which ended up looking like two big red gumballs on the Styrofoam's cheeks. She didn't forget about the lips either —they're blood red. The gold, hoop earrings looked like an afterthought or maybe by then Izzy was bored with her art project. *Who knows.* Only one of the earrings was actually *on* the earlobe. The other was drawn on the neck.

Needless to say, Grandma wasn't thrilled with the make-over at first. But when she heard our reactions upon seeing the new and improved head —terrified screams, including Dad's —she changed her mind and decided to keep the head "just for fun". Even now, every time someone opens the pantry, Grandma's chuckling somewhere nearby (even if no one is screaming).

I looked around for the chips Grandma wanted me to get. I didn't know what chips she had in mind —the open bag of stale nachos or the open bag of stale cheddar potato chips —so I brought both.

I was a little embarrassed by Grandma's sorry contribution but she didn't seem to be, of course.

"Put them over there," she pointed to a nearby table.

I noticed that beads of sweat were pouring down her face.

"Aren't you hot?" I asked, fanning my face with a paper plate.

"A little," she answered and wiped her face with a napkin.

I couldn't imagine wearing a hat in this weather. And that's exactly what a wig was —a furry hat!

"Grandma, you should take off your wig. It's too hot. You might get sick." I was worried.

"Nonsense," she replied, using her favorite word in the English language. *I think Grandma was wired to disagree.*

"It's really hot, Grandma," I insisted.

"I can't take the wig off," she said. "I might as well sit here in my underwear if I'm not wearing my wig."

I chuckled at the thought.

"Now how would *that* look?" she asked, chuckling herself.

"Pretty funny," I answered.

"Exactly," she said and wiped her face again. "Now where is that food you promised me?"

"Oh, yeah. I forgot. I'll be right back," I said and walked away.

When I came back with Grandma's food, she was talking to another neighbor. When Grandma saw me and the plate I was carrying, her eyes lit up. She took the plate from me, smiled, and said, "And this is my sweet Sofia."

Sweet Sofia? Me?

"I've heard so much about you," the neighbor lady said and smiled at me. "I was just telling your grandma how lucky she is to have her family living with her. I hear that you're a great cook too."

"Not really." I shook my head, a little embarrassed.

I looked over at Grandma and she was smiling at me and nodding, disagreeing with me, once again.

"Well your grandma says that you cook for her all the time." The woman kept smiling at me. I just stood there. I didn't know what to say.

"Sofia, why don't you go and get some food. You must be hungry," Grandma chimed in and off I went.

I got some food and came back to the house but since Grandma was still yacking away with that neighbor, I decided to sit on the curb in front of the house. I didn't want to chat with that woman.

I stared at my hamburger and thought about the block parties we used to have in Oak Park. Grandma Martha always joined us even though she didn't live on our block. Nobody cared. The idea was — the more people, the merrier. I started to miss Grandma Martha again but not in a depressing way this time. It was a happy sadness. That was weird.

"Why so glum?" Andrew sat down next to me.

I didn't hear him coming. "Glum?" I asked, surprised to see him sitting so close to me.

"Yeah. Glum. Is it because Maggie's leaving tomorrow?"

"Yeah…No…Well, yeah, partially. But also…my grandma is getting married," I explained.

"No way! Ursula? Who's the guy?" he asked and looked around as if trying to locate the groom on the crowded street.

"No, my other grandma," I corrected him.

"Oh. So why so glum?"

"Well, she's too old and I don't want another grandpa. Plus, now I'll probably never see her," I went down my list of negatives.

"Do you want her to be alone?" he asked.

"No." I answered quickly.

She has us, I thought. *Isn't that enough?*

"My grandpa's remarried," he informed me.

"Really?" *I don't know why I was surprised. I don't even know the guy.*

"Yeah. He told me once that he got married because he didn't want to live alone."

That's a lousy reason to get married, I thought. *I would never do that. I would only marry you for love, Andrew.* I looked at him with longing. Luckily, he didn't know what I was thinking.

"Old people get lonely, Sofia," he said and got up to leave.

So Grandma Martha was lonely? But we moved away only a couple of months ago. She didn't have to hurry up and find a husband the second we were gone. *That's just crazy.*

"Your grandma will still visit you, don't worry. And in the meantime, you still have this one," he said and pointed at Grandma Ursula.

"Yeah, you're right," I agreed.

"I know I'm right," he laughed. "I'll see you later."

"Yeah, see you later," I said and smiled.

I looked at Grandma Ursula sitting alone on the porch, eating her hamburger and wiping the sweat off her face. I thought about all the previous BBQs —before our invasion —after which she'd get up and go inside an empty house, with no one and nothing —except some lousy cabbage soup —waiting there for her. The thought made me sad.

When we first moved in and I mistakenly mentioned to Grandma that she might be too old to be swinging on her porch-swing, she explained, "I just can't help myself. It's a swing. You swing on a swing. It doesn't matter how old you are."

Today her feet were planted firmly on the concrete porch. She looked old.

For the first time in my life, I felt deeply sorry for someone *else*. *I'm not a self-absorbed person. I just don't go around feeling sorry for other people all the time.* And for the first time this summer, I was truly happy that we moved in with Grandma Ursula. *It's funny how a person sitting on a porch, chewing a burger, can make you realize all this.*

She looked up from her hamburger and our eyes met. She smiled at me and I started to cry. She threw her paper plate on the floor - hamburger and all —which was shocking, given Grandma's love of food, and rushed toward me. Well, it was more like a slow-motion movie. She careened toward me. Her housedress was flapping wildly in the wind but her wig, *that wig*, sat firmly on her head and not a single, fake, poop-color hair follicle dared to move.

This person, this solid wig, is my grandma.

"What's wrong?" she asked, all out of breath, with rivers of sweat pouring down her face.

"Nothing," I sobbed. "I love you."

Epilogue

Thank God this crazy summer is almost over! I can't wait 'til school starts. (I can't believe I just said that.) New teacher? Who cares! Don't know anyone at school (except for Andrew)? No problem. A deaf piano teacher who likes to stick tape on her face and other places? Everyone needs a hobby. A Grandma who...well, you know all about her. All I know is that the new school year has got to be an improvement.

CPSIA information can be obtained at www.ICGtesting.com
Printed in the USA
LVOW08s1822150913

352516LV00004B/408/P

9 780988 268500